DATE DUE

JA 8 '01	JA 04 '10	
JA 25 '01		
MY 14 '01	NR 02 '10	
OC 24 '01	MR 21 '11	
NO 05 01		
NO 20 '01	JAN 23 2012	
MR 05 '02		
JE 04 '02		
OC 28 02		
FE 9 '03		
FE 25 '03		
MR 13 '06		
NO 20 '06		
MR 13 '07		
AP 24 '08		

LAUREL-LEAF BOOKS

Careful, careful, little girl.
I'm keeping track of you.

Jennifer glanced down at the open drawer of the desk, at the jumble of letters and papers it contained. There were grocery receipts, old shopping lists, one of Bobbie's report cards, but a paper sticking out of the pile near the front of the drawer drew her attention. The scrawly handwriting looked vaguely familiar. It wasn't Bobbie's or Stella's. Why did she feel as though she ought to be able to identify it? The few words she could read made no sense. They came at the end of what seemed to be a short mailer about a sale at Dillard's Department Store. It wasn't signed. She picked up the paper and folded it in half, shoving it in the back hip pocket of her jeans. She wasn't supposed to touch anything, but there was something about this paper she had to remember. She'd bring it back later, and in the meantime it couldn't be important to anyone.

Jennifer jumped guiltily as Lucas suddenly appeared beside her, his mouth close to her ear. "Keep looking in the drawer," he said.

"What—?"

"Don't look up. Look—in—the—drawer. We've got a visitor outside. Someone's watching us from the yard beyond the back window."

Laurel-Leaf Books by Joan Lowery Nixon

THE HAUNTING
DON'T SCREAM
A CANDIDATE FOR MURDER
THE DARK AND DEADLY POOL
A DEADLY GAME OF MAGIC
THE GHOSTS OF NOW
THE ISLAND OF DANGEROUS DREAMS
THE KIDNAPPING OF CHRISTINA LATTIMORE
MURDERED, MY SWEET
THE NAME OF THE GAME WAS MURDER
THE OTHER SIDE OF DARK
THE SÉANCE
SEARCH FOR THE SHADOWMAN
SECRET, SILENT SCREAMS
SHADOWMAKER
THE SPECTER
SPIRIT SEEKER
THE STALKER
THE WEEKEND WAS MURDER!
WHISPERS FROM THE DEAD

THE STALKER

Joan Lowery Nixon

Published by
Bantam Doubleday Dell Books for Young Readers
a division of
Bantam Doubleday Dell Publishing Group, Inc.
1540 Broadway
New York, New York 10036

The trademark Laurel-Leaf Library® is registered in the U.S.
Patent and Trademark Office.

The trademark Dell® is registered in the U.S. Patent and
Trademark Office.

ISBN: 0-440-97753-3

RL: 5.1

Reprinted by arrangement with Delacorte Press

Printed in the United States of America

One Previous Edition

May 1992

OPM   19   18   17   16   15

To my friends,
Bebe Willoughby
and
George Nicholson

Acknowledgment

With appreciation for the assistance of
Sergeant Larry Olivarez, Corpus Christi
Police Department Community Services Division.

THE
STALKER

1

Through the late afternoon she sat alone on the steps of the seawall, listening to the gulls' cries and watching the boats bob and rock at their moorings; so she didn't know about the murder.

The breeze from the Gulf, pungent with salt and shellfish, had fingered her hair as she tried to decide what to do about Mark and knowing she should be reading her class assignment in the English Lit book that lay open in her lap.

Jennifer Lee Wilcox was a sunbrowned seventeen—almost eighteen—in the senior class of Corpus Christi High School, and the future was as mysterious and blank as the cloudy bay water that rose and ruffled against the steps below her feet. She loved Mark—she was fairly sure that she did—but she didn't want to go from a cap and gown to a wedding gown. Grannie kept saying she was lucky to find a nice boy like Mark; but Jennifer knew there ought to be something else in her life. There had to be more.

She was late getting home, and in her hurry she let the

wind tug the screen door from her fingers, clapping it against the weathered wood siding.

"That you, Jennifer Lee?" Grannie shouted over the blaring voices in the television set.

"Sorry I'm late, Grannie," Jennifer said. She pulled the door into place and latched it, hurrying through the small hallway into the living room, where Grannie stood before a rickety wooden ironing board. "I'll get supper started right away," she added.

Grannie pressed the remote control to flip off the set, then turned to stare at her, squinting over the cigarette that hung from her lower lip. Wisps of gray hair stuck out from the badly wrapped bun on top of her head, and she reminded Jennifer of a faded round pillow that was losing some of its stuffing. "Where ya been?" Grannie asked, adding before Jennifer could answer, "You haven't heard, have you?"

"Heard what?" Jennifer put her books on the nearest table and picked up a stack of her father's blue cotton work shirts. She was prepared to listen patiently to whatever new gossip Grannie had come up with, before she stacked the shirts on the shelf in her father's closet.

"That girl you spend so much time with," Grannie said. "That Bobbie Krambo."

"You always say that. Her brothers' name is Krambo. Bobbie and her mother's last name is Trax."

"Makes no never mind. The poor thing got herself murdered."

Jennifer could see Grannie, yet at the same time couldn't see her. There was a blue fog between them, and she could feel the shirts plopping against her feet.

"What did you do that for, girl! I spent an hour ironing those things."

Grannie bent to pick up the shirts, fussing at them as

she smoothed and folded again. Jennifer grabbed for the back of a nearby chair, anchoring herself, sliding into it, rubbing her eyes until the fog lifted.

"Bobbie was murdered?" she whispered.

"You look awful," Grannie said. "You want a glass of water or something?"

"No," Jennifer tried to say. She cleared her throat and began again. "No, Grannie. Just tell me about Bobbie. What happened?"

Grannie gave a last pat to the pile of shirts. "First of all, you got it all mixed up," she said. "That girl, Bobbie, didn't get murdered. It was her mother."

"But you said—"

"You didn't give me a chance to finish. What I was going to tell you was that Bobbie's the one who murdered her mother."

"She couldn't!" Jennifer jumped to her feet. "I don't believe it."

Grannie shrugged. "It's what the TV said."

"Who said it? What did they say?"

"Some bigwig in the police. They interviewed him, and he said she was a suspect."

"Being a suspect is different from having done it," Jennifer said. "I know Bobbie didn't murder anyone. What about those awful stepbrothers?"

"What about them?"

"You know, Grannie. One of them was even in prison."

"Don't ask me," she said. "I didn't even know they still lived in these parts."

"They don't. But they come here often enough."

Jennifer shuddered, picturing Bobbie's round, freckled face with its wide, ready smile. "Easier to laugh than cry," Bobbie had once told her. And "Fiddledeedee. To-morrow is another day."

"Scarlett O'Hara said that," Jennifer had reminded.

"I know, and that's the only thing she said or did that made sense. She was a big fool not to fall in love with Clark Gable."

"Don't scowl like that," Grannie was saying. She knocked a long ash from her cigarette into a saucer filled with twisted butts. "I'm only telling you what the TV said."

Jennifer took a long breath. "It's just taking me time to figure this out, Grannie. I don't know what to think except that Bobbie didn't—she couldn't do it."

"Long as you're up, take these and put them away." Grannie put the stack of shirts back into Jennifer's arms.

"Where is Bobbie? Did they say?"

"Good question. Police don't know where she is. Looks like she up and run away. Nobody on God's earth knows where that girl's gone off to."

Jennifer clutched the shirts to her chest, ducking into the smell of starch and scorch so that Grannie couldn't see her face. "I'll start supper," she mumbled, and hurried from the room.

Where was Bobbie? Suddenly, surely, Jennifer knew.

A few moments later Jennifer was leaning against the closet door, head pillowed on her arms, trying to sort out what Grannie had told her, when she heard Grannie yell, "Doorbell don't work, y'all." There was the sound of a muffled, deep answering voice, and Grannie's loud "Hold it. I'm coming."

In a matter of seconds Grannie shouted, "Jennifer! Come on in here! *Po*-lice want to talk to you."

Jennifer looked into the mirror over her father's dresser at the pasty-faced, big-eyed stranger who stared back at her. She moved to the mirror, leaning into it, rubbing her cheeks until the color came back, smoothing down the flyaway ends of her long brown hair, breathing deep and hard until she felt she could face whomever she'd meet in the living room.

"Jennifer Lee Wilcox! Where are you?"

She hurried into the room, rubbing damp palms down the sides of her jeans, and came to a halt, standing tall and steady before the two men who were waiting for her.

They wore ties with their sports coats and slacks, and little beads of sweat glistened on their foreheads. They looked like detective characters looked in the movies, with broad shoulders and flat stomachs. The tallest one pulled out a handkerchief, mopped his forehead, and introduced himself and his partner, but the names slid through Jennifer's mind like hot cooking grease through a sieve. She stood without moving, her eyes steadily meeting those of the man who had spoken.

"Please sit down," he said. "We'd like to sit down, too."

He dabbed at his forehead again, and Grannie said, "We save the air conditioner for the summer heat. Don't need to spend all that money in the fall when there's a good breeze comes up."

Jennifer obediently squeezed around the ironing board, careful not to jolt the tip-tilted iron that wobbled in place, and perched on a nearby chair, sitting as straight as its ladder back. The two men lowered themselves heavily onto the lumpy sofa, squashing the upholstered bouquets of spring flowers that had faded years ago.

The shorter detective, whose brown hair was lighter than his partner's, had the faint beginnings of jowls, and his sunglasses had dug creases in his cheeks. He pulled out a pad and pen and asked the first question: "You're Jennifer Lee Wilcox?"

" 'Course she is," Grannie said. "I told you so already."

The taller man nodded and seemed almost to smile. "All this has to be official," he said, as confidentially as though Grannie were a third partner.

She leaned back in her chair, satisfied. Jennifer said, "Yes, I am."

"You're one of Bobbie Trax's friends?"

"Yes."

" 'Bout her closest friend," Grannie added.

"You knew Estelle Trax?"

"Yes. Bobbie's mother."

"Nobody calls her 'Estelle,' " Grannie said. "They call her Stella."

"You know that Stella Trax was murdered?"

"She knows. I told her when she got home a little while ago." Grannie sat upright, blinking against the cigarette smoke that drifted upward from the corner of her mouth. "First she'd heard of it, too. She liked to have keeled over. Dropped all my fresh-ironed shirts."

The taller detective leaned toward Grannie. "We'll let them do the talking. You and I will just listen," he said.

Grannie smiled at him.

The men seemed to be waiting for her to say something, so Jennifer nodded. "It's the way Grannie said. She heard about it on the television news. She told me when I came in. Only they're wrong. Bobbie couldn't have killed her mother."

"Where had you been?"

"Didn't you hear me? I said Bobbie couldn't have done it. She's not the kind of person who would kill someone."

"Jennifer," the taller detective said, "it's our job to get information. We'd appreciate it if you'd just answer our questions."

"But I can tell you things about Bobbie that other people might not know. We're good friends. She talks to me about things that bother her. She laughs away a lot of her problems. She doesn't hold them inside and then blow up. She isn't like that!"

"We'll ask you about Bobbie Trax later."

"What about her stepbrothers? Maybe they did it. Elton's even been in prison, and Darryl is a real loser."

The detective who had been asking the questions put down his pen to mop his forehead again. "We'd appreciate it if you'd just tell us where you were before you came home this afternoon. It would help us all if you'd cooperate."

Jennifer gulped back the words she would like to shout at this man and took a deep breath. "I went to the seawall after school was out. I like to sit there and do my homework." A trickle of sweat rolled down her backbone. "It's cool there with the wind coming off the bay."

She expected a word of agreement, some response, but there was none, and she had to remind herself that this was an interrogation, not a conversation.

"You said that you and Bobbie Trax are good friends."

"Yes."

"You've been to her house often?"

"Yes."

"While her mother was there?"

"Yes."

"Then could you tell us something about their relationship?"

"Relationship?" Jennifer knew she must sound like an

echo chamber. She stammered, "I don't know what you mean."

"Did they get along with each other? Did they argue? How did Bobbie feel about her mother?"

How did she feel? How would anyone feel? Stella Trax had made it clear that motherhood was a pain and a bore. But Jennifer was not about to tell these detectives anything that might make things more difficult for Bobbie. "I don't know," she said.

The questions went on, sometimes circling back to those that had been asked before. A fly batted and buzzed against the ceiling, and the air was stale with heat. There were questions she would have liked to ask them: How did Stella Trax die? How did they know she was murdered? What made them think that Bobbie committed the murder? But there was a formality about these men that frightened her, that kept her from asking. So she sat there, calmly repeating her answers.

"When was the last time you saw Bobbie Trax?"

"Yesterday, at school."

"You didn't wonder why she wasn't in class today?"

Jennifer shrugged. "I supposed she was sick. A lot of kids have that twenty-four-hour bug. I was going to call her after supper to find out."

The taller detective pulled a small package from his coat pocket. Carefully he unwrapped the brown paper and took out a wrinkled scarf. It was red, with a wild-patterned design of rock musicians and notes. "Have you seen this before?" he asked.

"Yes," Jennifer said. "I gave that to Bobbie a couple of years ago. It was a joke—kind of a private joke between us, because Bobbie liked the drummer in that group and—"

"Thank you," he said as he folded the scarf and put it back into his pocket.

"Why did you ask me about the scarf?" With a shock like a slam between her shoulder blades, Jennifer knew what they would answer. Gasping, hurting, she stammered, "You haven't told me. How was Bobbie's mother murdered?"

Grannie spoke up. "The TV said she was strangled—with a scarf."

"That's the scarf? But it doesn't mean Bobbie did it! Anyone could have picked up that scarf! You're wrong about Bobbie if you think she murdered her mother!"

"Calm down," he said. "We're trying to gather facts to get to the truth. You can help us do this. Just sit back and take a couple of deep breaths and pull yourself together. We'll wait until you're ready."

Jennifer's breath came out in shudders, as though she'd been crying. She tried not to think, to make her mind a blank, until finally a gray numbness—like a thick fog creeping in from the ocean—crawled from her mind throughout her body. Her fingers unclenched and were still.

"Ready?" the detective asked.

"Yes."

There was a pause. The detective with the pad and pen leaned toward her just a fraction. The other one did, too. It was coming—the question Jennifer had expected, had been afraid of.

"Jennifer," he said, "do you know where Bobbie Trax is now?"

Jennifer looked at him without blinking, as steadily as she could manage. She gripped the arms of her chair so tightly that her fingers ached as she answered, "No, I don't."

2

It's hot. Sticky heat. Itchy heat. Head hurts. Maybe that's why my head hurts. The damned heat. Yeah. Think about the heat. Don't think about anything else. It happened, so it had to be. Don't think about it. What's done is done. Don't think.

Pure luck that the kid went out.

The heat smells like oily gluck from the ship channel. Maybe that's why my head hurts. Don't think. I guess it's good that I got in so easy, and no one but Stella was there. I wasn't about to let anyone get in my way.

Just one thing worries me. Where did Stella keep the stuff? I should have made her tell me. I suppose if it's hid that good it might never turn up.

But what if someday it does?

3

Jennifer stood at the screen door, watching the detectives' unmarked gray sedan wobble over the potholes in the street, brake lights blinking like two sore eyes. Beyond this street of small frame houses, marked with explosions of unkempt lavender and pink crepe myrtle bushes and wind-twisted water oaks, rose the uptown skyline of the city, the picture-postcard backdrop for the curving sweep of the bay. She had been born in Corpus Christi, and she liked it; liked the tropical shrubbery overflowing the yards; the breeze that consistently blew in from the sea; the sudden, drenching rainstorms; the weekend sailboats that dotted the water with small rainbows; and the heavy steamers that plodded through the channel, under the soaring bridge, into the harbor.

She knew this city well. But now she had the strange sensation that she had been moved to an unfamiliar place without landmarks, that she was lost and alone, and the terror of it made her tremble.

"Don't see how you can be cold in this weather, but

instead of just standin' there, shiverin', go put on a sweater." Grannie's voice, directly behind her, startled Jennifer so much that she jumped. "You did good, the way you spoke up nice and polite to those police," Grannie added. "I know you were feelin' real bad." The matter-of-factness in her voice broke the spell.

"Grannie, I've got to go out," Jennifer said.

Grannie's eyes narrowed. Jennifer didn't know if it was protection from her cigarette's smoke, or if she was trying to peer inside Jennifer's mind. "Who're you goin' to see?"

"Mark," Jennifer answered.

Grannie studied her another moment, then nodded, satisfied. "Go ahead. You had a shock. Mark will talk to you, help you feel better about what happened."

As Jennifer grasped the metal latch on the door, Grannie's tone changed, and a sigh skipped through her words. "Don't mind about fixin' supper. I'll just heat up some leftovers."

"Oh," Jennifer said, and she took a step back into the room. "I forgot all about supper. I'll make it."

"No." Grannie held her arm. "I said I'd do it. Just leftovers. No problem. Tomorrow night's different, though." She tucked her chin in and scowled. "That woman who works at the flower-plant nursery with your daddy is comin' by to supper."

"Her name is Gloria. I keep telling you that, Grannie."

"Makes me no never mind what her name is. We just got to put together somethin' nicer than usual for supper, or your daddy isn't gonna be happy."

"I'll think of something. Maybe pot roast." Jennifer hurried out the door and down the porch steps, leaving her grandmother's words for her own ears: "What he sees in that woman—"

It wasn't far to Mark's house. They even took the same route to and from school. Convenient. Maybe that's why they had started going together. A year ago he was a new tudent in school. He had suddenly appeared at her side s she ran down the steps of the red brick building, glad hat school was over for the day, and said, "I'll walk you ome."

She had stopped, looking up at him, interested because rom the moment she first saw him, passing him in the allway at lunch period, she had been well aware of his lond good looks. She was even more interested now, ecause his eyes were as warm as his smile.

"Do you know where I live, Mark?"

"I wanted to know, so I made it a point to find out." Ie paused. "You know my name."

"I wanted to know," she had said, and they laughed.

Now she needed to talk to Mark. And she needed his ar.

She found him where she thought he would be—in the arage, tinkering with the motor of his old moss-green Chevy that looked shrunken inside its four oversize tires, n a frame that lifted it high in the air.

He smiled as he saw her. He wiped his hands on the eat of his jeans and came toward her eagerly.

"You haven't heard about Bobbie's mother," she said.

"Bobbie's mother?"

"Sit down," Jennifer said. She pulled Mark to a patch of thickly tufted lawn next to the driveway, and she told him all that she knew.

When she'd finished, he kept staring at her. "Oh, God!" he said. "I didn't know."

"I need to borrow your car."

He blinked, bewildered at the change in topic. "What

for? I mean, I've got to be at the supermarket by six. I've got a late shift this week."

"I know you do, and you'll get to work on time. It's getting close to six o'clock now. I can drop you off. When the store closes I'll be there to pick you up. Okay?"

His mind had apparently clicked into gear, because he said, "You're going to wherever Bobbie is. Right?"

"Do I have to tell you?"

"No. You don't need to tell me. It's easy to figure out what you're planning. Did she call you?"

"No. I haven't heard from her."

"Then how do you know she'll be there?"

"I just know."

"Do you want me to go with you?"

Jennifer took his hand and held it. The strength in his fingers kept hers from trembling. "Thanks anyway, but I don't think you should. You'd get in trouble at the market if you didn't show up. Remember how rotten the manager acted when you were out with the flu."

"He's nothing but talk. He was shorthanded then and didn't care why I was out."

"I don't want you to go with me. I just need your car to get there."

Mark looked at his car, then back at Jennifer. "Okay," he said slowly. "But remember she goes faster than it feels like, so watch your speed. And if you put her into four-wheel drive the clutch still sticks a little, so when you move the stick through keep it slow and easy."

"Thanks," Jennifer said. She stretched up to kiss him lightly, automatically.

He patted her shoulder, but he was clumsy and awkward, and his touch was hard enough to bounce her forward, off-balance. She knew he was trying to tell her he understood that the fear she felt for Bobbie had flooded every particle of her mind, leaving no room for any other emotion. "Come on," he said. He stood, pulling Jennifer to her feet. "Keys are in the ignition. You can drive me to the store, and that way I can see how you handle her."

She knew how to drive Mark's car. She had driven it a couple of times before, and they both knew she was a good driver. But she patiently allowed Mark the ritual of trauma as he turned his prized possession over to someone else.

Jennifer pulled up against the yellow-painted curb in front of the store's wide glass windows and slid the gear into park. Inside, among the gaudy array of merchandise, customers, and signs, she could see the manager scowling at whoever dared to stop in this no-parking zone.

Mark had seen him, too. He opened the door on his side, stretching his long legs toward the ground and aiming his kiss somewhere near her right ear. "Good luck," he said; and as he shut the door and leaned his arms on the open window, he added, "Tell Bobbie—uh—tell her—"

"It's okay," Jennifer said. "Bobbie will know what you mean."

Smoothly she pulled away from the curb, steering this high-seated monster through the busy lanes of the parking lot, back to the street. She cut over to Padre Island Drive, glad for the open freeway and the way Mark's little car quickly picked up speed with just a slight touch to the accelerator. It was hard not to speed. Bobbie. She had to find Bobbie.

She crossed the Oso, that narrow tongue of water that licks inward from the bay. Across the flat, blue expanse, under the gray-tinged pile of clouds that were blowing in from the Gulf, she watched a needle-nosed silver plane glide to a landing at the Naval Air Station. The scene was

lazy and unreal, part of someone else's world. She kept
her eyes on the road. Careful now. Careful. Just a few
blocks through the poky traffic in the town of Flour
Bluff, then open road on the Kennedy Causeway, across
the Laguna Madre—its peaceful waters dotted with fish-
ermen—to North Padre Island . . . and Bobbie.

Weatherbeaten tourist stores—small wooden shelters
still piled with shells and printed T-shirts—were clus-
tered with late-night convenience markets and gas stations along the road. Jennifer slowed the car as she came
to Whitecap and followed the curving street to the strip
of condominiums that faced the open waters of the Gulf.
In the spaces between them she could see the rolling
green-gray surf and the empty stretch of white sand. Not
many people would be here. It was too late for the summer crowds and too early for the winter Yankees.

It would have been easier to drive down on the sand,
but she wanted to bring Mark's car back to him without
a spot on it. So she parked beside the last condominium
and climbed the dunes to the empty stretch of beach that
lay to the north.

The hard-packed sand at the water's edge was easier to
walk on, especially since she had to work against a steady
wind that blew from the sea. Jennifer took off her shoes
and ran, hair whipping across her face, ignoring the occasional foam that swept up the sand and over her feet,
splattering and soaking the legs of her jeans.

There was a special place she and Bobbie had found
last year, an old lean-to tucked back in the dunes and
abandoned, too far from the condominiums to be discovered by the people who stayed there, and too far to be on
the regular beach patrol. They had visited the spot often,
carrying in bags of sandwiches, potato chips, and Cokes;
snuggling inside the shelter, talking about guys and love,

letting the rhythm of the surf wipe out the problems they had brought in, too.

Sometimes they had hitchhiked to the island; sometimes one of them had been able to borrow the family car. But no one else knew about this place, not even Mark.

Jennifer kept a careful watch on the sand, jumping over an occasional purple blob. Even when dead, the Portuguese man-of-war had a poisonous sting. She was winded, gulping in great breaths of the damp, salt-packed air; more eager than ever to reach Bobbie.

And there it was ahead: the lean-to, its roof partially covered with a drift of sand.

Jennifer moved slowly now, fighting off the sudden thought that maybe she was wrong, that maybe Bobbie was far from here.

She stopped. "Bobbie?" The wind snatched her words, and she shouted again, pulling away a strand of hair that plastered itself against her lips, cupping her hands around her mouth. "Bobbie!"

There was a movement at the open side of the lean-to, and Bobbie crawled out, straw-yellow hair whipping around her head. She scrambled to her feet. "Hey! Jen!" she called. "What are you doing here?"

Jennifer stopped, taking long, deep breaths to steady herself, waiting for Bobbie to come to her. She knew it! Bobbie hadn't killed her mother. She didn't even know what had happened!

Bobbie stumbled through the loose sand and stood in front of Jennifer. "Hey," she said again, and smiled. "Don't look so miserable. Stella and I just had another shouting match, and I thought I'd stay away a couple of days." Her smile tightened as she added, "She won't miss me."

Jennifer reached out and grabbed Bobbie's arms. "Listen to me," she said. "Something terrible happened. I suppose there's a right way to tell you about it, but I don't know how."

Bobbie's eyes widened, fixed on Jennifer's, as she waited.

Jennifer pulled a strand of hair from her mouth, tossing her head against the wind. "It's about your mother."

She couldn't continue, and Bobbie said, "What about Stella? Did she get arrested? Is she sick? What?"

The words came out in a cry. "Somebody murdered her!"

"No." Bobbie shook her head, saying it over and over. "No, no."

Jennifer stepped forward, trying to hug her friend, but Bobbie moved backward, still staring at Jennifer. "How? Who killed her?" Bobbie asked.

"I don't know," Jennifer said. "And there's more."

"Do the police know who killed her?"

"Listen, Bobbie, I said there's more. Right now the police think *you* did it!"

She wished Bobbie would cry, would get angry, would feel something. But Bobbie was like one of the wood carvings in the museum. And her voice was flat. "Why?"

"Because it must have happened after you left your house. The police think you killed your mother and ran away."

Bobbie closed her eyes, and when she opened them something inside her had wilted. "I didn't. You know that. I didn't."

"Of course I know that." Jennifer wrapped her arms around Bobbie's shoulders. "That's why I'm here."

"What will I do?"

"I don't know."

"Maybe I should go to the police and tell them I didn't do it."

"I guess. As long as you hide out they'll think you're guilty."

"Yeah. Okay." But Bobbie began to shake. "What if they don't believe me? I'd like to get away from here. Maybe Mexico. I could hitchhike."

"That's no good," Jennifer said. "Don't worry. We'll find out who did this thing. I promise." She held Bobbie tightly until the shaking stopped. "Are you going to be all right?"

Bobbie nodded against Jennifer's shoulder. "Sure."

Jennifer was suddenly aware of the sand stinging her face. The wind had become stronger, and the water and sky were darkening, with tag ends of clouds out over the sea reflecting the pinks and golds of a hidden sunset.

"I've got Mark's car," she told Bobbie. "Let's go."

She felt Bobbie stiffen only an instant before she heard the shout from above the dunes.

"Don't move!"

Instinctively she released Bobbie and stepped backward, twisting to stare upward.

"Hold it! I said, don't move!"

Against the twilight sky stood four uniformed policemen, their pistols aimed at Jennifer and Bobbie.

4

Newseye Tonight. Good evening. Just a short time ago police apprehended, as an alleged suspect, the daughter of a local hairdresser who died last night after being brutally strangled. Police, who have booked the suspect, Bobbie Trax, an eighteen-year-old student at Corpus Christi High School, for the murder of her mother, Estelle Trax, refuse to release any further information at this time. We'll go to Margie White on film shot this afternoon in front of Estelle Trax's home in northeast Corpus Christi.

"Margie White here, and I'm outside the modest home where Estelle Trax's body was found today by her next-door neighbor, Mrs. Lila Aciddo.

"Mrs. Aciddo, how did you happen to find the body?"

"I—uh—don't know if I should—uh—"

"It's all right, Mrs. Aciddo. Just tell me what you told the police."

"Well, it was Stella's day off from the beauty parlor,

and she was supposed to—uh—come over so we could—uh—you know, go shopping."

"And—"

"She—uh—didn't show up and, well, after the fight yesterday—"

"What kind of a fight?"

"I told the police about it. That girl and her mother were shouting at each other so loud I could hear it, even with my window on that side of the house closed tight, because it got painted stuck. And then it was quiet, so I looked out the window, and I seen Bobbie—that's the girl—go out the front door and run down the block. I didn't think nothing about it then, because that wasn't the first time they had it out with each other. So this afternoon I guess I kinda thought I ought to make sure everything was all right and find out from Stella what happened, you know, and that's when I went over there, and looked in the back window, because the doors were locked, and it was awful."

"Thank you, Mrs. Aciddo. Today police are searching for Bobbie Trax who—"

I don't believe it. Crazy. It's darned crazy how things work out. Yeah, I heard them arguing, and I even saw that nosy old biddy come to the window and pull the drapes aside to get an eyeful. She didn't see me. None of them saw me. It was dark in those bushes back there by the garage. But all I had to do was wait, and then it was easy to get in.

Now the cops have their suspect.

I wouldn't have planned it like this. Couldn't have. Maybe they'll stick the kid with it. Maybe not. Depends on what evidence they've got. Depends on what kind of an alibi she can come up with.

Gotta think. Gotta get some aspirin to take care of this headache. Stupid kid. Who's it gonna be—you or me?

Let's see what I can do to make sure it's *you*.

5

"You through crying?"

Jennifer wadded the soggy tissue between her hands and glared at the detective who faced her across the narrow desk. The interrogation room was a small cubicle with tile walls that reminded her of the bathrooms at school. At her left was a glass partition open to a large room that held desks and rows of files and was decorated by two walls filled with bulletin boards. Now and then someone passing through the homicide department glanced in at her without curiosity.

"I cry when I get angry," she muttered.

"No point in getting angry," he said. "We just follow the book. That's the way things get done."

"It isn't fair!" she said. "Bobbie didn't even know what had happened! We were coming back to the city. We were going right to the police station to tell them she didn't do it." He didn't answer, and she added, "That was sneaky of y'all to follow me."

"We're not holding you," he said. He tilted back his

chrome and red-plastic chair and stretched, hands clasped behind his head. "Why don't you just go home and cool off?"

"I want to see Bobbie."

"Can't do that. She'll be arraigned—"

"What does that mean?"

"It means after she's interrogated here she'll be taken before the municipal court judge, charged with the crime, and then she'll be taken over to the county jail where she'll get charged, booked, fingerprinted all over again."

Jennifer shuddered. "You can't do that! Someone else killed Stella, not Bobbie!"

"Who?"

"I—I don't know." She leaned toward him. "You're the police. That's what you're supposed to find out!"

"We go by the book," he said. "We get evidence. We collect facts. They add up. They give us the answer."

"What facts? Just because Bobbie and her mother had an argument?"

"There's something called—well, I'll put it so you can understand it. When it's obvious that only one person has been with the murder victim, and there is nothing to suggest that anyone else has entered the scene through force or consent, then it's a pretty sure thing that the person who was on hand is the one who committed the murder."

"How do you know no one else was there?"

"Calm down," he said. "If you were a policeman you'd know that most murders happen between family members or friends. This was one of the easy ones."

"Bobbie isn't the kind of person who kills someone."

"You'd be surprised at some of the so-called nice people who suddenly lose control. Anyone can kill."

"I don't believe that."

He shrugged. "She'll be assigned a public defender,

and within a hundred and twenty days she'll get a fair trial. The jury will decide if she's guilty or not. Does that satisfy you?"

"But there has to be something else you could do to find out the truth!"

"There's no point in wasting man-hours on a case that's as obvious as this one. We've got other evidence."

"That stupid scarf. It's the only so-called evidence you've got, isn't it?"

He ignored her question, hefting himself from the chair. "Come on. I'll check you out of here."

He walked out of the interrogation room into the central room of the homicide department, Jennifer edging around the table to follow him.

"If you won't do anything to find who the real murderer is, then I will!" She spoke so loudly that a few people turned to stare at her. Her face tingled, and she repeated quietly, "I will."

One corner of his mouth turned up in a smile. "I don't think you'd get very far. Unless you've got a license as a private investigator and just haven't mentioned it."

"What would a private investigator do?"

He stopped abruptly, joining a cluster of men at one of the desks. He clapped a tall, gray-haired man on the shoulder. "Lucas! How're things going?"

The man was sitting-leaning against the edge of the desk as straight and thin as a hoe handle. He smiled easily. "Got to keep in touch," he said. "Someone's got to see if you boys are doing what you're supposed to do. Right?"

"Right! Good to see you around." The detective headed toward the hallway with long strides, and Jennifer hurried to catch up. "Lucas Maldonaldo," he said. "Retired a few months ago, and can't stay away. One of the best investigative officers ever. We all learned a lot from Lucas."

"Please—I asked you a question," Jennifer said. "I asked you what a private investigator would do to help Bobbie."

"Well," he said, "a P.I. would check into the scene, talk to your friend, to witnesses, and so on. He'd do about what we've already done."

"But he might learn something else."

"It's happened. That's one way they earn their keep." They reached a desk. He retrieved a manila envelope and handed it to her. "Here's your stuff. You'll find your boyfriend's car parked in the lot across the street."

Jennifer signed the paper he handed her, shook her watch from the envelope and put it on. It was almost time to pick up Mark. She'd better hurry. She shoved her wallet into the back hip pocket of her jeans and clutched the keys to Mark's car.

"I've got a girl about your age," the detective said. "Goes to Ray High. Plays a lot of basketball. Anyhow, I know you kids take things pretty hard, and this is a rough one for you." He blinked, looking uncomfortable. "I'm trying to say, don't tear yourself up attempting to make things come out the way you want them instead of the way they are. See what I mean?"

"I know Bobbie." Jennifer's words were spaced and slow, as though she were talking to a child who couldn't understand. "She didn't kill her mother."

She turned and left the station, running down the steps, crossing the nearly empty street to the parking lot, where she found Mark's car nosed in under one of the bright arc lamps. She drove it out of the parking lot and down the side street to Staples, heading toward the supermarket where Mark would soon be waiting for her.

Would a private investigator help? Why not find out?
She had some money—not much—but there was a small
bank account where she put something from the pay-
checks she got for her weekend and summer work at the
Green Garden Nursery. There was almost three hundred
dollars in the account now. And she'd be willing to spend
it all to help Bobbie.

She knew a private investigator. Well, she didn't really
know him. She had met him a year or so ago when she
was over at Bobbie's and some guy had come by to pick
up Stella for a date. They'd said hello, and after he and
Stella had left, Bobbie had told her the man was a private
eye. They had giggled about that and about his funny
name. What was his name? If she could only remember
it! She had never seen him again, and Bobbie hadn't mentioned him; so apparently he and Stella hadn't dated
much. But he knew Stella. Surely he'd want to help.

Mark came out of the side entrance of the market at
the same time Jennifer pulled to a stop next to the curb.
"Good timing," he said, climbing into the driver's side as
she quickly scooted over. "Did you find Bobbie?"

Jennifer told him everything that had happened as he
drove her home. She ended with her encounter in the
interrogation room as Mark parked his car in front of her
house. He turned off the ignition and twisted in his seat
to face her.

"You might have been shot!"

"But I wasn't. Anyhow, that doesn't matter. Bobbie
matters. We've got to help her."

Mark's scowl was made deeper by the shadows cast
from the streetlight. "That detective was right. Leave it
alone. They wouldn't have arrested Bobbie if they didn't
think she'd done it."

Jennifer gasped. She hadn't expected this reaction from

Mark. "But Bobbie didn't even know her mother was dead! I had to tell her!"

"A guy in the store said he heard on KRIS that the scarf that strangled Mrs. Trax belonged to Bobbie," Mark said. "Bobbie could have put on an act with you."

"Even if you don't believe in Bobbie, I do! And I'm going to do what I can to help her." Jennifer reached for the door handle, but Mark grasped her shoulders, turning her toward him.

"Right now you're upset. So'm I. But you've got to take it easy and slow and think things out. Maybe get away for a while." His voice softened and deepened. "Jen, I've got an idea, and please don't say no until you think about it. Why don't you and I go over to Padre for the weekend?"

"No."

"Look," he said. "I worked this all out and gave it a lot of thought. I know how you feel, but it won't be wrong. We love each other, and we're going to get married right after graduation. That's only a few months away. And you need to be comforted and loved right now."

"I haven't said I'd marry you."

"Not in so many words. But we've both taken it for granted all along. You've said you love me. You aren't changing your mind, are you?"

"No. Oh, I don't know!" She could feel the tears burn up to the surface again, and she cried out, "Mark, I don't know what I feel about anything right now!"

"See? That's what I mean." He was closer, enfolding her tightly in his arms. "You need me, Jen."

She struggled to sit up, pushing his arms away, rubbing at the tears with her knuckles. "Not that way," she said.

He shrugged and leaned back against the door, watching her. "Okay, then. How?"

"I'll—I'll let you know. Right now I don't know."

"When you do, just tell me. I'll be on hand," he said. "You know that, Jen."

She nodded, opened the door, and jumped down. She didn't watch Mark drive away.

The chipped pottery lamp on the corner table gave a yellowed glow to the living room. As Jennifer came through the door, she could see her father asleep in his chair, his chin tucked into his chest. The television set was still on. She turned it off, and her father awoke, snuffling a little, coughing as he sat up.

"I guess I fell asleep in my chair," he said.

"You do every night." Jennifer came to his side and smoothed down the strands of hair that curled upward at the back of his bald spot. "You work such long hours."

"We planted the front of that new mall on Everhart today. Got all of that part done." He blinked as though he were suddenly aware of his surroundings. "Oh, Jennifer! Mama told me about your friend Bobbie! I'm sorry, hon." He reached for her hand and squeezed it.

She squatted next to the arm of his chair, her face close to his. "Dad, what Grannie told you isn't true! Bobbie didn't do it! I promise!"

"Well now, hon," he said. "Hon—I—I hope not." He blinked again, looking confused.

Jennifer rested her forehead against his shoulder. She was too tired to go through this again. "Never mind, Dad. We'll talk about it tomorrow."

Jennifer awoke early, resentful of the fact that she had slept at all. The normal patterns of life seemed to be out of place. All the tooth-brushing, bed-making, breakfast-eating routines belonged to another, alien world. An empty coffee mug and a plate dusted with toast crumbs showed that her father had already left for his job. As usual, Grannie wasn't up yet.

Taking her orange juice and toast to the living room, Jennifer turned on the early news, catching a repeat of the interview with Mrs. Aciddo. "Bobbie didn't do it!" Jennifer muttered. "And I'm going to prove it!"

She wolfed down her breakfast, then opened the Yellow Pages. She didn't know where else to look for the information she wanted. If she saw that man's name, she'd recognize it. It was funny. Why? She couldn't remember. There was nothing under Private Investigators, so she looked up Detectives. She was surprised to find "Detective Agencies—Private." She supposed that she had expected secrecy, a covert, undercover method of discovering these people.

The name jumped out at her as she scanned the page: Bartlee Biddle. Of course. She jotted down his address.

Jennifer looked up the number of the attendance office at school. One of the student helpers should be there now. She dialed it, and when a voice answered she gave her name and said, "I'm not coming in today."

The voice said in a rush, "Jennifer, we all know about Bobbie. And you were practically her only really good friend, and it must be awful for you, although I guess you could have expected it with a mother like Bobbie has—had."

"Look, Alicia," Jennifer said, recognizing the voice, "you're only supposed to take the messages, not give opinions."

"Well, if you're staying out because you're upset about

Bobbie, I can understand it. That's all I'm saying. Shall I put down that you're sick, or what?"

"I don't care what you put down. Okay?"

"Okay, okay. I'll say you're sick, so they won't get on your case. Gotta hang up."

There was a click before Jennifer could put down the receiver. She sat in the kitchen chair, her hand still on the phone. So Bobbie didn't have many friends. Neither did Jennifer. They weren't in the popular group, they didn't have time for all sorts of school activities. Some of the girls didn't like Bobbie because she got kind of noisy at times, and used too much makeup, and dressed in all the wrong colors and wrong things; but Jennifer didn't care because Bobbie made life fun and full of laughs, and when Jennifer really got to know Bobbie, she found a steady, kind, and loving person, a good friend. Lately she hadn't seen as much of Bobbie as she used to, because of the time spent with Mark; but Bobbie hadn't seemed to mind.

Jennifer had never cared to have a lot of friends. She felt comfortable with just a few people, and that was the way she wanted it. She had Bobbie and Mark to spend time with, and a few kids to talk to in each of her classes. She didn't need more.

But she did need Bobbie, and it was time to get busy.

The phone rang, and she grabbed for it, hoping it wouldn't wake Grannie.

"Jen," the voice said. "It's me—Darryl."

"Darryl?" Jennifer was so surprised, she didn't know what to say. "Uh—do you know about your mother, Darryl?"

"Yeah," he said. "They got in touch."

"I—I'm sorry about what happened. I—"

"That's why I called you."

The pause that followed felt like an empty hole that had to be filled. Jennifer stammered, "Uh—Bobbie told me last week you were in Arizona with your dad. Are you in Arizona now?"

"Got to Corpus a few minutes ago. Trailways bus. Jen —about Bobbie."

"She didn't do it, Darryl."

"Are you her alibi?"

"No. But she didn't do it."

"How come you're so sure?"

"Because Bobbie's my friend. I—I'm the one who found her and told her what had happened. She didn't know."

"Big innocence, huh? Could of been an act."

Just what Mark had said. Jennifer gripped the receiver and tried not to shout at Darryl. "You're her stepbrother. You're family. You ought to trust her."

"No law says I have to."

"Look, she gave me her word."

"Just her word. So she hasn't got an alibi. That's what I needed to find out."

"Are you going to help her?"

"Nothing I could do. Nothing anybody could do."

"Yes, there is," Jennifer said. *"I'm* going to help Bobbie. I'm going to hire a private investigator to find the real murderer!"

Without waiting for his answer she slammed the receiver on the cradle. Stupid pothead! Darryl was one of the most obnoxious guys she had ever met. She shouldn't have expected him to lift a lazy finger to help Bobbie. He was a loner, a drifter, a loser. She wished he would just go back to Arizona. She never wanted to talk to him again!

She finished getting dressed, closed and locked the

front door quietly, and set off for the bus stop. She was going to see Mr. Bartlee Biddle, private investigator, specialist in family matters, child custody, and divorce. The "family matters" ought to cover it—and the fact that he once dated Stella.

Mr. Biddle's office was down the street from the courthouse in an old brick building with wood trim that badly needed painting. There was no elevator, so Jennifer climbed worn wooden stairs to the third floor.

Near the head of the stairway she could see a door with Mr. Biddle's name stenciled on it. As she reached for the doorknob, the door suddenly opened and she nearly collided with a man so lean and limber he gave the impression that his bones were held together with binder rings.

"Oh!" Jennifer said. "Sorry." The man, who was dressed in a dirty T-shirt and tight jeans, paused, staring at her from under a battered cap he had pulled low on his forehead. He didn't speak. As the question in his eyes slipped into boredom, he moved aside and clattered down the stairway.

"Jerk," Jennifer muttered under her breath, and entered Mr. Biddle's office. A battered desk stood near the window. It was cluttered with papers covered in large, scrawled handwriting. Some were puckered with dried brown coffee rings, and the wastepaper basket next to the desk overflowed in a crinkled white eruption. On a dirty tray at the far end of the desk were a hodgepodge of paper clips, chipped coffee cups, and a jumbled assortment of nonprescription drugstore remedies. A fat, balding man in a sport shirt with wide, moon-shaped stains under the arms suddenly reared up from behind the desk, heaving himself to his feet.

Jennifer jumped and took a step backward.

"Dropped some papers down here," he said. "Been meaning to clean this mess up, but things have been busy."

Jennifer took another step toward the door.

"Don't go away," the man said. "You must have come here for some reason. What can I do for you?"

"You—you probably don't remember me," Jennifer stammered. "I—I met you about a year ago. You had come to pick up Mrs. Trax for a date. I was with Bobbie. We said hello. I mean, you and I said hello."

She was so nervous, she couldn't help babbling. His eyes had narrowed as he studied her, and he didn't speak. "What I'm here for," she finally said, "is—well, I'm looking for a private investigator."

"Why?"

Jennifer took a gulp of air, forced herself to walk up to Mr. Biddle's desk, and said, "Let me start over. I didn't even tell you my name. I'm Jennifer Lee Wilcox, and I need someone to find a murderer."

Mr. Biddle's head shot up, his jowls quivering. "You better go to the police, young lady."

"The police have arrested the wrong person. They think my friend murdered her mother, and I need someone who can find out who really did it. Since you knew Mrs. Trax, I thought you'd want to help."

"Stella Trax," he said so softly that at first Jennifer thought he was talking to himself. "Your memory's better than mine, young lady. That was a long time ago, and I don't remember you at all." He lowered himself into his chair and stared at her until Jennifer squirmed. She really hadn't expected him to remember her. Adults never remembered kids.

"Well?" she finally asked. "Can you help me?"

"Nope," he said. He picked up a wad of papers and

tapped them against the desk top, trying to straighten them. "So I dated Stella once. Makes no difference, because I don't handle cases like that. My specialty is divorce—finding out who's up to what, and getting pictures. That's about it."

"I've got to find somebody to help me," Jennifer said.

He chuckled. "Whoever you go to, it's going to cost. You know that?"

"Of course."

"You're sure?"

She didn't like the mocking twinkle in his eyes. "I want to hire an investigator. I wouldn't expect not to pay."

"Okay, then, since you've got a few dollars, you might try Crandall and Kline. They've got an office in that new Towers Building over on Upper Broadway near Mestina. Think you can find it?"

"I know the building," she said. She wasn't sure if she should take him seriously. He seemed to be making fun of her.

He shoved a pad of paper and stubby pencil toward her. "Write down your name, address, and phone number," he said. He stared at her for a moment, then added, "In case."

She quickly scribbled the information on the pad, then stood up and looked at him. "In case? Does that mean you might help?"

"No," he said, ripping the sheet from the pad, folding it, and tucking it into his shirt pocket. "But you never can tell what might turn up."

That taunting look was still in his eyes; so without another word to him, Jennifer turned and left his office.

It was only a few blocks to the Towers Building. This was a trim, modern structure with a sleek, mirrored facade, and a lobby floored and walled in black marble as cold as the arctic air that spewed from the air conditioner. A glassed-in wall directory gave the Crandall and Kline number on the twelfth floor, and an elevator door opened at her touch on the panel.

This office was plain, but neatly carpeted and decorated in blues and beige. Even the receptionist at the front desk matched the decor with her pale hair and light blue blouse. "May I help you?" she asked with such a friendly smile that Jennifer's story tumbled out.

"Mr. Crandall and Mr. Kline will take a murder investigation case, won't they?" she finished.

"Oh, my, yes," the receptionist said. "But Mr. Crandall is out of town, and Mr. Kline has an appointment in fifteen minutes." She added hopefully, "Perhaps you'd like to make an appointment?"

Jennifer eagerly leaned on the desk. "I could tell him in *five* minutes! Really I could! Only five minutes of his time, if he'll just talk to me!"

The receptionist began to frown, then abruptly seemed to change her mind. "Well, we'll give it a try," she said cheerfully. "Sit down over there, and I'll find out."

Jennifer obediently perched on one of the straight chairs at the side of the room, holding her hands together so tightly her fingers hurt, as the receptionist spoke into the phone in a voice so low that Jennifer couldn't hear what she said. Finally the woman raised her head and smiled. "Go ahead, through that door on the right," she said, adding, "Good luck!"

The man who came to meet Jennifer was around forty and trim in neat slacks and a sport shirt. He shook hands with Jennifer and smiled as she stammered her name. "Please sit down," he said. "Can you tell me your story as quickly as you told it to Sandy?"

"Yes," Jennifer answered, so intent she was unable to

return the smile. Remembering that five-minutes promise, she took even less time than when she had told her problem to the receptionist.

Mr. Kline made a steeple of his fingers, pressing them against his chin as he thought. The room was silent, except for the tick of a small wooden clock on a corner table. Finally he sat upright and said to Jennifer, "I agree with you on two points. First, there have been cases in which private investigators have uncovered evidence crucial to a case, which the police have overlooked. And second, I am also of the opinion that certain personality types would be highly unlikely to commit murder."

Jennifer perched on the end of her chair, so excited she could hardly breathe. "Then you'll help me?"

"I'll talk it over with my partner when he gets back to town tomorrow, and I'll call you."

"Oh, thank you!" Jennifer cried. "Thank you!"

Mr. Kline smiled. "Will Bobbie's family pay for the investigation? If so, I should meet with them, too."

"Oh. Oh, no. I'll take care of it," Jennifer said. "Bobbie doesn't know where her father is, and her two stepbrothers wouldn't do a thing to help her."

"You'll be able to handle it financially?"

Jennifer took a long breath. "I guess I'd better find out what an investigation will cost."

"It's pretty standard," Mr. Kline said. "Investigators are paid by the day. Most of us charge seventy-five to a hundred dollars a day with a retainer up front to cover expenses. In this case a five-hundred-dollar retainer ought to be enough."

Jennifer closed her eyes, fighting down the sick feeling in her stomach. "Oh, no," she murmured.

"I'm sorry. I didn't hear what you said."

"I haven't got that much money." Jennifer looked into

Mr. Kline's eyes, hoping—she supposed—that a miracle would happen.

"Perhaps we could arrange an extended payment plan."

"It wouldn't work," Jennifer said. "I don't have nearly enough money. It would take years for me to earn the rest."

Mr. Kline swiveled his chair so that he was facing the window, his back to Jennifer, who was trying to breathe normally. Finally he turned and got to his feet. "I hope you understand, Jennifer, that I am sympathetic to your friend's problem. But this is a business, and I have a responsibility to my partner and his family as well as to our employees, and—Well, I just can't afford to take this case without remuneration."

Jennifer swallowed hard. It hurt her throat. Somehow she managed to get to her feet and heard herself thanking Mr. Kline for his time. She shut the office door behind her, nodding to Sandy, who was chatting with Mr. Kline's next appointment.

As she waited for the elevator, she rested her head against the wall. There had to be an answer! There must be someone who was a good investigator who would help her.

A good investigator. The best investigative officer ever.

She could see the man who had leaned against the desk in the homicide room at the police station. She remembered his smile, his easy manner. She even remembered his name: Lucas Maldonaldo. Retired. Wanted to keep his hand in.

She heard the hum of the elevator approaching, and she straightened. Maybe. Maybe. There must be a telephone directory in the lobby of this building. She could look up his telephone number. No—his address.

If Lucas Maldonaldo was as good a policeman as the detective had said he was, then he would want to find out who really had murdered Bobbie's mother.

It wouldn't hurt to try.

Less than an hour later Jennifer stood on the small front porch of a pink brick home in a tract on the south side of Corpus Christi. The scraggly crepe myrtles on each side of the house were still in bloom, and the bed of deep red mums seemed to fight against the clutching tendrils of Saint Augustine grass that should have been cut back.

She could hear footsteps as someone came to answer the bell, and she nervously wet her dry lips with the edge of her tongue, hoping—praying—that she would say the right words.

The door swung open, and she looked up at the man she had seen in the homicide department.

The light, inquisitive smile that had deepened the lines at the edges of his dark eyes lasted only a moment. His look became penetrating, and Jennifer realized that he had recognized her, too.

Before he could speak, she quickly blurted out, "Mr. Maldonaldo, I need you to find a murderer!"

6

She's like a gnat. A small nuisance. Brush it away. Slap at it. Why should she get in the way? It's not her business. It was over and done with. It should stay that way.

I'll be aware of what she does. I'll be watching.

For her sake she better not become more than just a nuisance.

7

Lucas Maldonaldo didn't answer. His eyes—the gray-black color of Grannie's battered skillet—drilled into her mind as though they could explore her thoughts without speech. Jennifer stood a little straighter, trying to match his stiff-backed posture. If he thought he could intimidate her by staring at her, he was wrong.

Finally he said, "You want a private investigator. I'm just a retired police officer."

"I don't have enough money to hire a private eye," she said. "The detective at the police station told me you were the best investigative officer he ever knew. That's why I'm here."

A corner of his mouth twisted in a wry smile. "I see. You can't hire a P.I., so you came to me. You think my services come at cut-rate prices?"

Jennifer shook her head. "No. If you've been a good detective for so many years, then there's something in you that wants to see the right person tried for a crime, not the wrong one. I came to you because I think if I tell you about Bobbie, you'll want to help me."

There was another long pause, until finally he said, "Come on inside. I'll hear what you have to say."

On the surface the living room seemed to be tidy, but Jennifer noted a thin layer of dust on the tables and on the array of small figurines that covered the top of an upright piano.

Lucas Maldonaldo's glance followed hers to the figurines. He had been holding a small bottle of aspirin, and he placed it on the piano lid next to a full-skirted china balloon-seller.

Jennifer glanced at the aspirin bottle. "If you've got a headache—I mean, I don't want to bother you, and—"

"No headache. Just one of the penalties of growing older. Arthritis," he muttered.

"I'm sorry." Flustered, she tried to change the subject. "I like your figurines." She carefully picked one up and examined it. "They need dusting."

Jennifer wished she hadn't spoken so bluntly, but he didn't seem to mind. "They're not mine. They were Lila's, and I can't seem to get around to all the housecleaning she used to do." He motioned to a chair. "Lila was my wife," he said.

Jennifer perched on the edge of a deep, upholstered chair, waiting until he slowly lowered himself onto the sofa across from her. "Mr. Maldonaldo, I'll tell you about Bobbie," she said.

He nodded agreement, so she went through the story from the time she had gone to the island until they had been taken to the police station.

"That's all of it," she said.

"No, it isn't," he answered. He leaned forward, elbows resting on his knees, and began to question her.

"Where are her brothers? How much do you know about them?

"What kind of relationship did Bobbie have with her brothers? With her mother?

"Had her brother Darryl ever been convicted on a drugs charge? When? Where does he live?

"Has Bobbie ever used drugs?

"What was Bobbie's schoolwork like? What grades did she make?

"Did she have an after-school job?

"What were her plans after graduation?

"Had she ever been in trouble at school? Ever arrested?

"Was she in touch with her father?

"When did she last see him?

"Did her mother have a boyfriend? A live-in boyfriend?

"How did Bobbie feel about the men in her mother's life?"

The questions went on and on, all of them delivered in the same firm, quiet tone that demanded nonemotional answers scraped from the bottom of her mind. At last he leaned back against the plump sofa cushions; and Jennifer, numb as though a skinned place had finally stopped throbbing, sighed with relief.

"You weren't aware that you knew so much about your friend, were you?" he asked.

"Or *didn't* know," Jennifer added. "You asked so many kinds of questions. Most of them didn't have anything to do with the murder. I can't see how they'd help."

"They helped me get a better idea of the situation," he said. "A murder doesn't just happen. There's a background to it, events leading up to it, personalities involved. This information gives a total picture."

He stood up, stretching a little, rolling his left shoulder as though it were stiff. "Next step," he said. "I'll talk to Bobbie."

Jennifer quickly got to her feet. "You'll help me?"

"I don't know yet," he said. "I'll decide after I talk to Bobbie."

"But you might? You'll really consider it?"

"I'll consider it."

"Because you believe in Bobbie?"

"At the moment," he told her, "I believe in *you.*" He fumbled through the papers in a nearby desk drawer, finally finding a clean sheet. "Here," he said, handing it to her. "Write down your phone number and address. I'll get in touch with you as soon as I make up my mind."

Jennifer was so excited, she passed the supermarket on Staples and had to backtrack to get the groceries for dinner. Grannie was right. Dad did want things to be special tonight. She counted the grocery money she had folded and stuffed into the back pocket of her jeans—not enough to make a bulge—and decided to go for chicken with that mandarin orange sauce. She had found the recipe in a magazine a few months back and made it, and Dad had been enthusiastic about it. And—let's see—brown rice, a green salad, broccoli—maybe string beans.

By the time she got home, Grannie was fretting at the open doorway.

"Well, thank goodness you showed up," Grannie said. "I thought you plain forgot about that woman coming for dinner tonight."

"Gloria," Jennifer said. She edged past Grannie and

heaved the heavy pair of grocery sacks to the counter top in the kitchen.

"Whatever," Grannie said. She stubbed out her cigarette in a nearby saucer. "She's kind of prissy, I think. Prissy and sure as heck not good-lookin' enough to stop traffic."

Jennifer washed her hands and got busy with the chicken. Grannie pulled up a kitchen chair.

"You didn't notice I fixed a bouquet of my yellow chrysanthemums for the table."

Jennifer looked up and smiled. "It looks nice, Grannie. Really nice."

"Don't want that woman to think I don't know how to make things look good when company's comin' over."

"Gloria," Jennifer said, still smiling. "Dad will appreciate the flowers. He likes Gloria a lot, you know."

"I know."

Grannie looked like a child who'd been sent up a dark stairway to bed. Jennifer wiped her hands on her apron and went to her, bending so that her head was on her grandmother's level. She took her by the shoulders and said, "Hey, Grannie, Gloria's a nice person. She'll like you a lot if you give her the chance."

"I've made my home with Roy ever since your mother died."

"Don't you know he's glad to have you here?"

"Maybe. But I don't know how that woman will feel about it if he's fool enough to ask her to marry him. Lots of women don't want another woman in their house."

Jennifer hugged her grandmother. "Don't worry about it now," she said. "Everything will work out all right."

But as she finished the dinner preparations and changed into a dress in Gloria's honor, she wondered how she could say that. People spent a lot of time telling each other that things would work out, that everything would be okay. How did they know? How did anyone know? You had to make things come out, make them happen, not just wait and hope for the best.

Why didn't Lucas Maldonaldo call?

She started as her father came into the kitchen. Gloria trailed him like a bright banner with her ruffled fuchsia blouse, hennaed hair, and wide smile outlined in crimson.

"Everything looks nice, hon," her father said. He didn't look tired tonight. He looked like a boy waiting for Santa to show up.

From the corners of her eyes Jennifer saw Grannie peering around the kitchen doorway. "You can thank Grannie for the flower arrangement," she said. "She really knows how to make things look pretty."

As Gloria exclaimed over the flowers, Jennifer heard a satisfied snort from the direction of the doorway.

"Can I help you dish up?" Gloria asked.

"Sure," Jennifer said, handing her a bowl and a spoon. "Would you put the rice in here?"

"Humph!" muttered a voice from the other side of the door. "She'll be doin' that soon enough."

"Yes, Grannie, it's soon enough to dish up," Jennifer said quickly, trying to override Grannie's words. She clattered the food into bowls and kept up a running conversation while the bowls were being put on the kitchen table. She shepherded her grandmother into a chair at the table and sank into her own, noting that nothing had dimmed Gloria's glow or her father's bewildered joy.

The telephone rang just as Jennifer picked up her fork.

"I'll get it," she said, sliding from her chair so quickly that she nearly knocked it over.

"If it's Mark, tell him to call back after you eat," Grannie said, but Jennifer knew it wouldn't be Mark.

"Hello?" It was hard to breathe as the voice she had hoped for answered.

"This is Lucas Maldonaldo, Jennifer."

"Yes?" she asked and could only repeat, "Yes? Yes?"

"I talked to Bobbie," he said.

"Is she all right?"

"She's a little scared, which is natural, and she isn't too happy about being jailed."

"Did you—?"

"Give me a chance," he said. "Calm down and listen."

"Okay. I'm sorry. It's just that I've been hoping—"

"I said, 'listen.'"

There was a pause that stretched like a rubber band to its limit. Jennifer closed her eyes in agony.

"I talked not only to Bobbie but to a couple of detectives who are assigned to the case. They're coming down on Bobbie because it looks like a natural. But there's a chance you might be right, that someone else killed Bobbie's mother. I told them so, and they think I'm off base, but they'll cooperate with us in giving us access to whatever information we'll need from the department."

"Oh!" Jennifer shouted. "Then you'll help Bobbie!"

"We'll help Bobbie," he said. "There's a lot of hard work involved in any investigation, and this will be a particularly tough one. We haven't got much to go on. I'm going to need you to work with me."

"Of course I will! Anything!"

"I'll see you tomorrow."

"Early tomorrow! I'll be at your house right after breakfast!"

"No, you won't," he said. "You'll go to school. Come by when your classes let out. If I'm not there, sit on the porch and wait for me."

"I could skip school."

"No," he said. "If we're going to do this, we're going to do it right." He added, "You might learn something at school besides what you'll learn in your classes."

"You mean about Bobbie and her mother? But what?"

"That's up to you to find out," he said. "Ask questions, and above all, pay attention to the answers. Listen. Remember it's often not what someone says, but how he says it."

"Well—" she said, not too sure what he meant.

"We'll talk more about it tomorrow," he said. "I hope you're a good student, because you've got a lot to learn."

"I'll work hard," she said. "And thank you, Mr. Maldonaldo! Thank you!"

"By the way," he said, "they've finished the autopsy, so Stella Trax's funeral is set for Friday morning at ten. Will you be there?"

"Oh," she said. "The funeral. Day after tomorrow. I hadn't thought about a funeral. Of course. Yes, I'll be there. Will Bobbie—will they let Bobbie come?"

"Her lawyer thinks the judge will give permission."

"Bobbie has a lawyer?"

"Everyone gets a lawyer. It's in the Constitution."

"Is he good?"

"He's a young fellow, not long out of law school. I don't know much else about him."

"Oh, Mr. Maldonaldo! He has to be good!"

"Jennifer, if we do our work well, it won't make any difference if he is or he isn't. The courtroom's not like a Perry Mason TV show. The lawyer doesn't suddenly come up with a guilty party. The information is collected before the trial ever begins, and that's where we'll come in. If we find the evidence we want, there won't be a trial." He paused. "Get back to your dinner. I'll see you tomorrow."

"Good-bye," she said. She continued to stare at the phone even after the connection had been broken. How did he know she'd been eating dinner? She heard the clatter of forks against plates at the table behind her and smiled. Apparently he had learned to listen. That's something she'd have to learn, too.

She sat at the table, tucked her paper napkin back on her lap, and shared her smile with the others. She realized that they hadn't said a word while she had been on the telephone. Now they'd want an explanation. I'm learning to listen, even if it's in retrospect, she thought, and she told them about the work she'd do with Lucas Maldonaldo.

"It's like in a movie!" Gloria said. She took a deep breath, and her ruffles rippled like a wavelet swelling and breaking against the shore.

"I wouldn't want you to do anything dangerous, hon." Her father's eyebrows dipped into a frown.

"It won't be dangerous, Dad. I'll be gathering information."

"That's what they do on those TV shows," Grannie said. "But those girl private eyes are always getting shot at or kidnapped or something."

"Nobody's going to shoot at me," Jennifer said, although she realized she knew nothing about what being an investigator would be like.

"I'm not sure about all this," her father said. "I don't know if I should let you get involved."

Jennifer sat up straight. "Dad," she said. "I'm going to help Bobbie. I'm not asking if I can do it. I've got to do it."

"Oh," he said. "Well." His voice was raspy, and he coughed a couple of times to clear his throat. "I guess it's all right. I guess that policeman fellow will take care of you."

Jennifer picked up her fork and knife and attacked the now cold chicken leg that lay under a pale orange mound of congealing sauce. Gloria began talking about a spy movie she had seen, with Dad nodding enthusiastically, as though his neck were a loose spring, and Grannie poking in sharp-tipped comments whenever Gloria paused for breath.

But Jennifer's thoughts were like stragglers that had finally decided to form a neat line. And the line led to one thought she hadn't faced yet. She and Mr. Maldonaldo were going to look for a killer. Whoever he was, he had killed Stella Trax. If he thought they were going to find him out, wouldn't it be logical that he'd try to kill again?

8

I can't stop worrying about it. The stuff. Maybe Stella didn't have any, and that's why I couldn't find it. It's obvious her kid didn't have it, or it would have made the news.

Dumb. It's dumb to worry about it.

This headache is bad. It makes everything worse. That's why I won't worry. Of course Stella had it.

But where is it?

9

There was nothing remarkable about Thursday morning, which was so ordinary it was horrifying. The sky was the same brilliant blue, its clouds handpainted a little too brightly white, the sun warm against Jennifer's back. The constant breeze from the south carried the heavy fragrance of overblown flowers from the red and pink oleanders that lined Ocean Drive, and people went about their business as though this were just another day.

As though nobody cared.

"*I* care," Jennifer said aloud, and she ached at having to go to school, to follow a routine that seemed to deny that anything more important had taken place.

She shifted her books in her arms as she approached the high school, and took a long breath. This was a waste of time. It was stupid! How could she accomplish anything here?

A gangly boy, who had begun too quickly to grow into his years, stood under one of the cottonwood trees. As

Jennifer approached, he stepped onto the walkway to join her.

"Hi," he said in a voice that split into two registers. His pimpled face reddened, and he stared at the ground as he tried again. "I don't think you know me. I'm a freshman. I—just—well, I've seen you at Bobbie's house, because I live near her, and—"

Jennifer wanted to shake him away, to hurry off where she wouldn't have to hear what he had to say, but she remembered she was here to listen; so she stopped on the walkway and waited.

But he gulped as though there was nothing more to say. Finally he stammered, "I guess I needed to say to somebody that I'm sorry about what happened with Bobbie and her mother. You're her friend, so I—"

Again he stopped in midsentence. Jennifer wanted to cry out that what he felt didn't matter, and run—just run away from all this. But she took a deep breath and asked, "You know Bobbie?"

"Kinda, I guess. We said hello a couple of times. We weren't in the same grade."

"She didn't kill her mother."

"The newspapers said she did."

"I don't care what they said!" Jennifer made herself calm down and added, "Did you know her mother?"

"No. Just saw her around. And my mom went to her for haircuts a couple of times when Mrs. Trax used to work at LaSalon, down on Chaparral."

Jennifer reached out and grabbed his arm, surprised at the sinews that tightened under her fingers. "Were you around on Tuesday? Did you see anything that might help Bobbie?"

"Take it easy," he said, his eyes widening. "I was playing basketball in the gym."

"When?"

"I don't know. I mean, I came home and found out from my mom about the murder." He took a step backward, shrugging out of her grip. "Look, I just wanted to tell you I'm sorry. I thought you'd be—well, I didn't know you'd get mad at me."

"I'm not mad," Jennifer said, but he had turned and headed toward the school in long lopes, like a frightened ostrich.

"This is just the beginning," she whispered to herself. Swallowing hard, to keep the tears from coming, Jennifer went to her first class.

During the day people stared at her, and as she passed through the hallways she left a wake of murmurs.

She was? Did you know? Really? Her friend. Did you hear? Her mother.

Some of the people she knew came close, hunching into her space, concern in their eyes as they said, "Good God! When I heard about it I nearly died! Jen, I'm sorry!"

"Bobbie didn't do it," Jennifer repeated over and over as the sun-shadows shifted from east to west. "You know that, don't you?"

"Jen, I didn't know Bobbie very well. None of us did."

"Look, Jen, I saw her every day in class, but that's about it."

"She really didn't want to be friends. You know that, Jennifer."

"I honestly think," Alicia said just after the last class ended, "that you were her only friend, Jen. Face it, Bobbie is kind of—well—different. *You* may think she wouldn't kill her very own mother, but *we* don't know that. We don't know anything about her at all!"

So as soon as school was out, Jennifer, struggling under a load of hurt too heavy to bear, dumped her books onto the Maldonaldo coffee table and her problems onto Lucas Maldonaldo himself.

"It doesn't matter what anyone believes," he said. "What matters is what you've found out today."

"Nothing," she said. She rubbed furiously at her eyes, as though she could grind the tears to a stop.

"What questions did you ask?" He shifted in his chair and stuffed a small pillow behind the curve in his back.

"Questions?" She looked up, startled. "There weren't many to ask. Nobody really knew Bobbie. Alicia said I was Bobbie's only friend, and she was right."

"Are you sure?"

"Well—yes. I mean, if Bobbie had any other friends I would have known them, wouldn't I?"

"Would you?"

"They would have been at school."

"Oh?"

Jennifer jumped to her feet and walked to the end of the living room and back. "Are you just trying to make me angry?"

"I'm trying to make you think."

"I am thinking."

"No, you're not. You're reacting. Now, sit down."

Jennifer immediately plopped back on the sofa. She fished into her handbag, pulled out a wrinkled tissue, and blew her nose.

"Start with the first person you met and talked to today. Think."

"Okay, okay. The first person was a guy who stopped to talk to me about Bobbie."

"Good. What was his name?"

"His name?" Jennifer shook her head. "Oh, no! I didn't ask him. He just said he was a neighbor of Bobbie's, and he didn't know her well, but he said his mother knew Bobbie's mother."

"Why did he talk to you?"

"He said he just wanted to tell someone he was sorry about Bobbie and her mother."

"Will you see him again at school?"

"I don't know. He's a freshman. That's all I know about him, except that he plays basketball."

"And he lives in Bobbie's neighborhood. Those are two facts that will help you find him in case we need to talk to him again."

"But he said he didn't know anything. He told me he was playing basketball and when he got home his mother told him about the murder."

"That's all he said?"

"That's all, Mr. Maldonaldo. Honestly."

"It takes too long to say 'Mr. Maldonaldo.' Call me 'Lucas.' " He stretched in his chair, hands clasped behind his head, his elbows poking out like sharply bent chicken wings. "Now, you've learned lesson one, Jennifer. Get names, get addresses, get facts, and write them all down."

"Everything? Even stuff that isn't important?"

"How will you know what's going to be important and what isn't until all your facts are gathered?"

Jennifer shrugged.

"Keep a small notebook with you, something you can carry in your purse."

"Okay."

"A lot of what a private investigator does is nitty-gritty stuff, looking up information in county and city record departments, in credit unions, state offices, and so forth. Getting that information is the background to investigations. So . . . get that notebook."

Jennifer nodded impatiently. "Aren't we going to go out and talk to someone or do something?"

"Yes," he said, "but slow down. First, I've got some information to share with you." He picked up a small notebook covered in imitation black leather, flipped a few pages and studied it. "Elton Krambo was released from prison on parole two months ago. He regularly reports to his parole officer in San Antonio. As far as the officer is concerned, Elton's come up clean."

Jennifer sat upright. "But it isn't far from San Antonio to Corpus Christi! He could have been here and his parole officer wouldn't have known about it!"

"That's right."

"So why don't you tell the police and have him arrested?"

"On what evidence?"

"On—well, he's a rotten person, and—Damn! You make everything so hard!"

He slowly put the notebook back on the table. "You want to give up?"

"No," she said. "I'm sorry. I didn't mean to sound off. I'm just impatient."

"I know you're impatient, and it's the worst thing you could be. Impatient people miss important facts. Impatient people charge into a case without getting sufficient evidence. Sometimes impatient people get killed. Do you get my point?"

"I couldn't miss it."

Lucas picked up the notebook and again thumbed through the pages while Jennifer clenched her teeth and her hands and tried not to shout.

"As for Darryl. You told me he had come in from Arizona early Wednesday morning on a Trailways bus. Right?"

"That's right."

"There were no early Trailways buses from Arizona or any points west scheduled for Wednesday-morning arrival. Are you sure he didn't say he'd arrived the night before?"

"I'm positive!" She stared at Lucas and added, "Darryl was lying, wasn't he?"

"Please don't tell me that now he ought to be arrested," Lucas said. "Just think of this as one more item to be checked out."

"But he lied."

"Lots of people lie. There are pathological liars, and people who lie to be evil, and people who get involved in all sorts of small lies for no particular reason. Or maybe they're scared, or trying to cover something not even related to the case. Or maybe they just find it hard to tell any story straight."

"There you go again!" Jennifer leaned forward, gripping her knees. "We're never going to get anything done if you keep giving me all these lectures!"

"We'll get something done," he said. "We'll find out who murdered Bobbie's mother, and we'll do it the right way."

"I—I don't know what the right way is."

"That's what I'm trying to teach you. As it stands now, you're a walking hazard—to me as well as to yourself. You've got your safety catch off and you're about as safe to be around as a loaded gun."

Jennifer sagged. "I'm sorry, Lucas."

Lucas heaved himself to his feet. "Remember what I've been telling you. Let's go."

Jennifer stood. "Go where?"

"I've got permission to go inside the Trax house. We're going to look—not touch, just look."

"Okay!" Jennifer scooped up her books so quickly she dropped some of them and had to scramble to pick them up. "What are we going to look for?"

"We don't know. One thing I've found, over and over, is that murderers are not as clever as they think they are. They'll make a mistake. Maybe they'll leave some clue."

"I don't understand. You mean like fingerprints?"

"It might be a fingerprint, or a strand of hair. It might be a blade of grass, or a bit of mud from his or her shoes."

"Something that small? How will we know it if we see it?"

Lucas's smile tipped one corner of his mouth. "This is what I've been trained to do. It's why you came to me for help. Right?"

Jennifer's cheeks felt as though she'd been too long in the sun. "I keep saying all the wrong things. I'm sorry."

"You'll learn," he said as he fished his car keys from his pocket. "Come on."

As they parked in front of the small frame house, Jennifer shuddered. In her eagerness to actually do something, she hadn't thought how hard it would be to walk into the room in which Bobbie's mother had been murdered. The living room was a vivid poster in her mind: yellows and lime greens and faded browns and muddied blues, old and lumpy upholstery dotted with a hodgepodge of pillows, none of which matched each other or anything else. A monstrous mismatched armchair stood in the corner nearest the entry to the kitchen. Two limp potted plants rested on a blond oak coffee table that looked like a reject from a garage sale. A metal magazine rack stuffed with *People* and *US* and outdated copies of

TV Guide was jammed against the wall. And a cluster of colored snapshots of Stella—a much younger Stella—framed in plastic, hung next to the light switch by the front door.

There was a special lock on the door, but Lucas had a key for it. He opened the door, stepped inside the room, and Jennifer followed him. She was trembling so hard she had to hold the doorframe to steady herself.

"Back door and front door across from each other," Lucas said.

"It's not a very big house," Jennifer said. "There are two bedrooms off to the right, and the kitchen is to the left."

Lucas slowly moved around the perimeter of the room, and Jennifer could see that a small, braided rug had been shoved aside to make way for the faint chalk marks that must have outlined Stella's body as it lay on the dull wooden floor.

"Oh," Jennifer said. "I think I'm going to—to—" She slid along the doorframe until she was sitting on the floor, watching the room twist and blur and pulse toward her.

"Go ahead and faint if you want to," Lucas said. "You'll come around soon enough."

Jennifer took a sharp, angry breath and blinked as everything snapped back into focus. "You don't even care? You'd just let me lie here?"

He turned to glance at her. "You don't look faint to me," he said. "I don't think I have to worry about you. Why don't you get up and see what you can do to help?"

Jennifer scrambled to her feet. She tried to think of something clever and cutting to say, but Lucas broke into her thoughts. "We need your memory now. Take a good, long look at everything in this room. From what you told

me, you've been here often enough to know if anything is
out of place."

"That end table," Jennifer said. "It's fallen over." She
automatically stepped toward it to straighten it, but Lucas's voice was sharp.

"Don't touch a thing! The table probably went over in
the struggle."

"Oh." Jennifer gulped. She stared at the room as
though she didn't know where to start.

"When you came to see Bobbie, which door did you
usually use?"

"The back door."

"Then carefully walk to the back door—this way,
around the edge of the room." Lucas waited until she was
standing at the closed door, then said, "All right. Turn
around and look at the room again. See anything that
doesn't belong? Anything out of place? Take your time.
People tend to remember only the most obvious details. I
expect better from you."

Jennifer took a long breath and began to study the
room from left to right. Nothing different. Nothing. But
something bothered her, and her glance swept back and
up. "Some of the pictures are gone," she said.

Edging the room again, she went to the wall by the
front door. The framed snapshots were like a bunch of
grapes with a few juicy ones plucked from the middle.
"Yes," she said. "There was a picture here, and here, and
over here. See—where the wall is a lighter color."

"Who was in the pictures?" Lucas was beside her.

Jennifer shrugged. "I have no idea. Mrs. Trax, of
course, but I don't know who else. I guess these must be a
collection of snapshots of her with her friends. This looks
like a picnic at the beach. And here's one taken in a
nightclub." She poked at one of them in the top row.

"Husband? Boyfriends?"

"Maybe. I guess. Bobbie might know. I've never paid much attention to the pictures, because I didn't know any of the people in them."

Lucas was writing in his black-covered notebook. "Okay," he said. "That was a good start. Anything else?"

She studied the room again, and this time she shook her head.

Lucas had opened a drawer of the table against the wall.

"I thought you said we couldn't touch anything," she told him; then she saw the pencil he had used to hook the plastic drawer pull. He didn't answer. He used the end of the pencil to poke through some of the papers in the drawer.

"How did the killer get in?" Jennifer asked.

"There was no sign of forced entry," he said. "Both doors were locked."

"What about the window with the broken lock?"

Lucas stood and looked at her sharply. "What window?"

Jennifer pointed to the window behind the sofa, the window opening to the backyard. "The window doesn't lock. The catch has always been broken. Bobbie sometimes used to slide it up and climb through when she forgot her key."

"Did anyone besides Bobbie know about the broken catch?"

"I guess. Her brothers must have known."

He was already at the window, bending, stooping, staring.

"Are you looking for fingerprints?"

"The window hasn't been dusted for prints," he said. "I'll get someone to do that."

"Will they let you know what they find?"

"We're not playing a game," he said. "We're not seeing who are the winners or the losers. We're all working for one thing—to gather as many facts as we can to help solve this case."

"Well, in detective shows on TV—"

"Forget what you've seen on television. It has nothing to do with life."

"Could we turn on a light?" Jennifer asked. "It's getting dim in here."

"We're almost through." He was bent nearly double, one hand pressing against the small of his back, as he studied the upholstery directly under the window.

Jennifer glanced down at the open drawer of the desk, at the jumble of letters and papers it contained. There were grocery receipts, old shopping lists, one of Bobbie's report cards, but a paper sticking out of the pile near the front of the drawer drew her attention. The scrawly handwriting looked vaguely familiar. It wasn't Bobbie's or Stella's. Why did she feel as though she ought to be able to identify it? The few words she could read made no sense. They came at the end of what seemed to be a short mailer about a sale at Dillard's Department Store. It wasn't signed. She picked up the paper and folded it in half, shoving it in the back hip pocket of her jeans. She wasn't supposed to touch anything, but there was something about this paper she had to remember. She'd bring it back later, and in the meantime it couldn't be important to anyone.

Jennifer jumped guiltily as Lucas suddenly appeared beside her, his mouth close to her ear. "Keep looking in the drawer," he said.

"What—?"

"Don't look up. Look—in—the—drawer. We've got a visitor outside. Someone's watching us from the yard beyond the back window."

10

There is no way the girl can connect us. I'm careful. Very careful. I know how to protect myself. And I know what to do with people who become dangerous to me.

Careful, careful, little girl.

I'm keeping track of you.

11

Lucas stood slowly, cautiously, wincing a little. Jennifer could see that although he seemed to be interested in what she was doing, he was gazing through the corners of his eyes at the window and whatever was beyond it. She wondered how he could be so calm. She wanted to panic and scream and run from the house, but fear shuddered through her body and she couldn't move.

"Jennifer, suppose you see what you can find in the kitchen." Lucas spoke in a normal tone.

"The k-kitchen?"

The firmness in his voice was a support that stiffened her back and propelled her legs into the cramped little kitchen. She didn't turn on the light. There was enough light coming into the room from the living room. She wanted to do as Lucas had told her, but instead she collapsed into the nearest chair, clinging to its wooden rungs as though in some way they could protect her. Jennifer tucked her feet up as a large cockroach scuttled across the floor and under the refrigerator. She glanced across the room to the telephone that balanced on top of the counter, as though it could automatically summon help. Maybe she'd have to call for help!

Lucas was a blur streaking across the room. The back door slammed, and someone screeched. Jennifer couldn't stand the suspense. She ran to the door, opened it, and peered into the darkness.

Limping toward her, into the patch of yellow light that patterned the grass, came Lucas. He was gripping the arm of a woman whose face was screwed into puckers of fear, propelling her against her will into the rectangle of light. Jennifer recognized her. She was one of Bobbie's neighbors, the one who had been interviewed on television.

"She lives next door," Jennifer said. "It's Mrs. Aciddo."

"I—I saw the light on," Mrs. Aciddo said. Lucas had let go of her arm, and she rubbed it, staring at him. The corners of her mouth turned down even more deeply. "You had no call to grab me. I got rights. Who are you? You're not even a policeman, huh?"

"We're investigating Mrs. Trax's murder," Lucas said.

Mrs. Aciddo stopped rubbing her arm and pointed at Jennifer. "You and that girl? Don't tell me that. She's a kid, that's all. She's got no business here."

"She's my partner."

Jennifer stood a little taller and sucked in her breath. That sounded good. It sounded right. "Mrs. Aciddo," she said, "we're trying to help Bobbie."

"Why? Anybody who kills someone deserves what they get."

"But Bobbie didn't kill her mother."

"I'm the one heard the fight." She tilted her head and looked coy. "You see me on the TV? They interviewed me. On Newseye. They showed it the next morning, too. I got to see it."

Jennifer nodded. "I saw the morning rerun. You said you heard Bobbie and her mother fighting."

"That's right. I heard it, and the girl ran off."

"But couldn't someone else have come to the house afterward?"

"I didn't see no one come."

"Were you looking?"

Mrs. Aciddo's lower lip jutted out. "You tellin' me I don't know what I seen or heard?"

Lucas stepped forward. "Mrs. Aciddo, we're sure your testimony will hold up with the police and the court. We're just asking if there could be something else that was missed, like someone else coming to the house—maybe after you went to bed?"

She shook her head stubbornly. "I didn't go to bed for a while after that. I was watching the TV."

"Someone could have come to the Trax house while you were watching television."

She shrugged. "Huh. I guess."

"Or afterward, while you were asleep?"

"I don't watch everythin' that goes on around here! I'm not a nosy neighbor!"

Lucas nodded. "I'm sorry. You seem to have a good eye for details. I thought you could help."

Her eyes became little slits as she studied him. "What do you mean, help?"

"There are some questions I'd like to ask you. Like, has either Elton or Darryl Krambo been here in the last few days?"

"Oh, I can tell you that," she said. She gave a heave of her chest, tucking back her chin, until she reminded Jennifer of the pigeons that strutted along Sherrill Park. "Elton never came around. Stella would have told me if he did, and there's been no sign of him since—since she was murdered. But that Darryl, he's been here. Oh, yes. Came to my house last week, rang my doorbell, and wanted to borrow some money."

"From you?" Jennifer gasped.

She was sorry immediately, because Mrs. Aciddo scowled. "Why not me? I've got a little money to use when I want. Everybody knows I'm not poor."

"I didn't mean it that way," Jennifer said. "I just meant that people usually borrow money from family members, not neighbors."

"Darryl would borrow money wherever he could get it. That kind needs money bad."

"That kind?" Lucas prompted.

"That kind on drugs," she said. "Stella wouldn't give him money for drugs. Even one night when he needed somethin' so bad he was sweatin' and shakin' and makin' a big fuss, she wouldn't give him money. She didn't like him messin' with drugs. She got on him hard for that."

"Did you see him Tuesday?"

"No." She looked disappointed. "Tuesday he could have been here, I guess. I was busy gettin' ready to go shoppin' with Stella. It was her day off at the beauty parlor."

Something made Jennifer feel uncomfortable. She wasn't sure what had nudged her, but she asked, "What beauty parlor?"

Mrs. Aciddo suddenly turned to Lucas. "I can't stand out here all night. If you're not the police, you can't make me."

"That's right," he said. "You can go home."

She took a couple of steps, and Jennifer came down the

wooden steps after her. "Please tell me, Mrs. Aciddo. Where did Mrs. Trax work?"

"How should I know?"

"You were her neighbor, her friend. You went shopping with her. She must have told you where she worked. Is there some reason you don't want to tell us?"

Mrs. Aciddo's short fat legs moved quickly, and Jennifer hurried to keep up. " 'Course not. I told you everything you wanted to know. Right?" She paused and mumbled, "Maybe Stella worked someplace on Chaparral, I guess."

"LaSalon?"

"Maybe. I'm not supposed to know everything about her. Now, go away and leave me alone. I'm missing my good TV shows, thanks to you and that man who is not a policeman."

Jennifer returned to the back steps and followed Lucas into the house. When he had closed the door, she said, "I remembered something. It may not mean a thing, but it's —well—peculiar."

He turned to listen, so she added, "That guy who talked to me about Bobbie at school, the one whose name I didn't get—" She stopped, embarrassed again, but Lucas merely nodded, so she said, "He told me something about his mother going to Stella to get her hair done when she used to work at LaSalon."

"Used to work?"

"Yes, and Mrs. Aciddo acted so strangely when I asked her where Mrs. Trax worked. Why would she lie?"

"Make a note," he said. "That's one of the things you can find out."

Jennifer had already pulled a small notebook and pen from the pocket of her jeans. "I'll go to LaSalon tomorrow," she said. "But—"

"What's your question?"

"I don't understand how Mrs. Trax's job means anything at all in how or why she was murdered, and I don't understand why Mrs. Aciddo should lie about where Mrs. Trax worked."

"That's what detecting is all about," Lucas said. "Lots of questions, lots of answers. They start fitting together like pieces in a puzzle."

"It's frustrating." Jennifer sighed. "I'd like it better if we could just find the murderer right away."

"Like in the movies where you'd open a door and there he'd stand, with a gun pointed at you?"

"You are so aggravating!" Jennifer said. "I didn't mean that at all. I—I don't know what I mean."

"Then suppose we get back to work. Want to check the bedrooms?"

"Not really," Jennifer said. "But I will." Reluctantly she entered the hall that connected the two small bedrooms. The door from the living room was near the door to Bobbie's room. The bathroom door was in the middle of the hallway. Jennifer decided to start with Bobbie's room and work her way down the hall.

The bulb was missing from the naked fixture in the hall, but it didn't matter. She flipped on the light in Bobbie's room. The room looked as it always had. The headboard of the bed, the chest of drawers, and the small desk and wooden chair had long ago been painted white. Now they were as yellowed and chipped as old piano keys. The corners of the worn, faded rose corduroy bedspread were neatly tucked in place, but the room was bare of mementos. With the exception of Bobbie's notebook and textbooks on the desk, there was nothing to show who lived in this room. Jennifer shuddered. The room always looked the same, but the sorrow of it had never reached her before. Why did Bobbie keep her room so bare?

Jennifer shook her head. Now she was behaving like Lucas with his endless questions. She went down the hallway to the bathroom, stepped inside and thought what a contrast it was to Bobbie's clean room. The cracked mirrored door to the medicine cabinet hung open on one hinge. Bottles were strewn on the ledge and the sink. A couple of towels lay on the floor, and there was a sour smell, as though someone had been sick.

Jennifer, trying not to gag, quickly stepped back into the hall. Yuck! What a mess! Shouldn't someone come into this house and clean it up?

Although the door to Bobbie's bedroom had been open, the door to Stella's room was closed. With trembling fingers Jennifer slowly turned the knob. She had no right to pry into the privacy of the woman who had lived here. After all, Stella had been her best friend's mother. Although Jennifer had often been in this house, she had never been in Stella's bedroom. It was a personal place, a—

She groped for the light switch, since the thin light that filtered from the living room wasn't strong enough to do more than create shadows. But her hand froze, and she barely managed to clutch the doorframe to steady herself as a shape detached itself from behind the bed, rising with a groan.

Jennifer screamed as it lunged toward her and collapsed in a sour, ragged heap at her feet.

Lucas appeared, roughly elbowing her aside and muttering, "Be quiet!" as he bent over the body.

"I thought—It looked like a monster. I mean, coming out of the dark like that—"

"Call an ambulance," he said. "Do you know how?"

"Well, of course I do!"

"Then move it!"

She quickly did as she was told, muttering to herself because he was treating her as he would a child. She stomped back to the bedroom and snapped, "I called your ambulance."

"Good," he said. "Do you know who this is?"

Lucas had rolled the man on his back. His eyelids were closed, one of them centering a deep purple bruise. His breath shuddered through swollen lips, and clumps of vomit had matted and dried on his unshaven chin.

"It's Darryl Krambo," she said. "He must have been in a fight."

Lucas grabbed the edge of the mattress and heaved himself to his feet. "Stay with him," he said. "I've got a phone call to make."

He left the room, and Jennifer stared down at Darryl. Any sympathy she might have felt for him was washed away by a rush of anger. "Lucas is going to call the police," she said to Darryl, not caring that he couldn't hear. "And you're going to be arrested for killing Stella, and I'm glad it turned out to be you, because you're a no-good junkie. You're a filthy, stinking—"

Darryl opened one eye, which rolled around crazily for a moment until it focused on Jennifer. He mumbled an obscenity.

Jennifer jumped backward, banging an elbow against the wall.

"I didn't kill Stella." The words oozed through his lips like soft butter through a cracked plate.

Lucas stepped into the room. "He's conscious?"

"Yes," Jennifer said.

Lucas sat on the edge of the bed, staring down at Darryl. "The ambulance will be here soon."

"I didn't kill Stella."

"No one's accusing you."

Jennifer tried not to look guilty as Lucas gave her a quick glance and continued. "Someone beat you pretty badly. Who was it?"

Darryl didn't answer. He closed his eyes and groaned.

"How long have you been here?"

"What's it to you? I live here."

"No, he doesn't!" Jennifer interrupted, but Lucas frowned at her, shaking his head.

Darryl groaned again. "I need a fix."

"Was someone here with you?" Lucas asked. "The person who beat you?"

Darryl mumbled something to himself, then apparently decided for some reason to answer the question. "I came here to be by myself." Tears rolled from his eyes, making paths down the scum on his face. "I need something bad," he said.

In the distance Jennifer could hear a siren. She hoped it was the ambulance. She was eager to get rid of Darryl and the smell and the horrible ugliness that made her want to gag.

"Do you know who killed your mother?" Lucas asked. His voice was suddenly soft.

"Stella—wasn't—she was my stepmother, not my mother."

Lucas looked at Jennifer, who could only shrug in surprise.

The siren was loud now. The ambulance was turning into their street. "Tell me who killed Stella," Lucas said, but Darryl groaned and turned his head away.

"Let them in the front door," Lucas said to Jennifer. She could hear footsteps on the walk, so she hurried to the door and opened it as the men arrived on the front steps.

It didn't take long for the ambulance attendants to strap Darryl into their folding stretcher and carry him back to the ambulance.

As the men left, Lucas followed them to the door, shutting it behind them.

"Is Darryl going to die?" Jennifer asked.

"I don't know. That's the doctor's job, not mine."

"You don't think he murdered Stella?"

"No, I don't."

"So we cross him off the list."

"Wrong. We put him near the top of the list. Who beat him? Why? Did the person who beat him intend to kill him? Why? What was Darryl doing in Corpus Christi?"

"Mrs. Aciddo said he was asking people for money to buy drugs."

"A side issue. What was he really doing here?"

"You ask so many questions, and there aren't any answers!"

"There are answers if we find them." He looked at his watch. "Your family will be worried about you if you don't get home soon."

"Are we finished here?"

"For the moment. We might come back."

Jennifer felt like crying. "We didn't find anything that would help."

"Weren't you paying attention?" he asked. "For one thing, you may have found the entry the killer used."

"Oh! The window."

"There were a few grains of dirt on the sofa, under the window. They could have been left by Darryl, but they could also have come from the shoes of the person who murdered Stella."

"Or the person who beat Darryl?"

"He wasn't beaten in this house. There were no signs of the kind of fight he'd have been in. No blood. It looks like he came here after his beating." He glanced toward the grouping of photos on the wall. "You're also forgetting the missing photographs."

"What good is something that isn't there?"

"If Bobbie can remember who was in the missing pictures, we might find out who didn't want to be recognized."

"You mean it might be the killer? But with so many pictures missing he covered himself, didn't he?"

"You'd be surprised how these things add up," Lucas said.

"I just thought of something," Jennifer said. "Didn't you call the police? They didn't come."

"That's because I told them to meet Darryl at the emergency ward of the hospital." He gave one last look around the room. "That's where I'm going now. I'll drop you off at home first."

He drove to her house as though he had been there before. Jennifer, wondering if he had checked her out and irritated because he must have done so, couldn't keep the sarcasm from her voice. "You know everything, don't you?"

"No," he said calmly. "For one thing, I don't know the identity of Stella's murderer. But if we both work hard at the job, we'll find out."

"Sorry," Jennifer mumbled. "I don't mean to be rude. I just feel like—Oh, I don't know how I feel!"

"It's stress," he said, "and you've got to learn to handle it."

He got out of the car, and she fumbled with her books, trying to climb out quickly. "Where are you going?"

"To meet your father." Lucas started up the walk.

"He's not home yet. And anyhow—"

"Then I'll introduce myself to your grandmother."

Jennifer stopped in the middle of the walk, unable to catch up with him. "Oh, Lucas, maybe it would be better if you didn't talk with Grannie."

He looked at her the way Miss Grabel in the fourth grade had looked when she discovered Jennifer was sneaking bites of her lunch instead of working on the history test. He turned and strode toward the front door.

Without a word Jennifer hurried to join him. She opened the door and Grannie shouted from the kitchen, "Jennifer Lee Wilcox! Come on in here and tell me why you're so late!"

Jennifer sighed, then walked into the kitchen, dumping her books on the table. "I had stuff to do, Grannie," she said.

Grannie waved a potato peeler like a baton. A cigarette wobbled on her lower lip. "You could of remembered that I've got enough to do without fixin' all the meals around here. At my age, I need your help, and it seems to me that—"

Lucas came into the kitchen. Grannie squinted to peer at him, and Jennifer quickly said, "Grannie, I'd like you to meet Lucas Maldonaldo."

"I'm glad to meet you, ma'am," Lucas said.

"You from the school or what?" Grannie continued to study him.

"I told you about him, Grannie," Jennifer said.

"I'm a retired policeman," Lucas added. "Jennifer asked me to help her friend Bobbie Trax."

"How you goin' to help her? Get her out of jail? Not much chance of that, far as I can see."

"Jennifer and I are trying to find the identity of the

person who murdered Stella Trax, and I want to reassure you that Jennifer will only be doing research and investigation with me."

"You talk as stiff as you stand," Grannie said. "My cousin Will stands like you do. Touch of arthritis. Right?" She didn't pause for an answer, adding, "Just put all that in plain English so's I can understand."

"I'm telling you that Jennifer shouldn't be in any danger."

Grannie rubbed her chin, her eyes widening. "I didn't like this in the first place. And now you're talkin' about danger."

"The work I'm giving her is routine. If I thought she'd be exposed to any danger I'd handle this myself. She'd be out of it."

"Wait a minute—" Jennifer interrupted, but Grannie held up a hand.

"Hush up, Jennifer," she said. "I need to find out more about this."

As though he was used to making clear-cut summaries, Lucas outlined what they had done and some of the things they planned to do.

When he had finished, Grannie leaned back against the sink and sighed. "Sounds like too big a job to me. I don't know why the police can't handle it themselves."

"Sometimes another viewpoint helps," Lucas said. He looked at his watch. "I've got to meet a friend at the hospital. If you or Jennifer's father have any questions, please call me."

"Don't know what good it would do. When she gets her mind set—"

Jennifer walked Lucas to the door as Grannie continued a muttered conversation with herself. "Are you going to Stella's funeral tomorrow?" Jennifer asked him.

"I'm not sure now. Probably. If you go, pay attention to who else is there. And afterward try to stop by the beauty parlor and find out if and when Stella quit her job there. I'll get in touch with you late in the afternoon, and we can compare notes."

"Okay," she said. "And thanks for coming in. You were right."

"No need for thanks," Lucas answered. "We've got a job to do, and if you pay attention and learn what you need to learn, we'll do it."

She didn't watch him go down the walk to his car. She shut the door and leaned against it. Sometimes he made her so angry she wanted to yell at him. If there were anyone else who could help. But Lucas seemed to be the only one. She straightened and shoved her hands into the back pockets of her jeans. The fingers on her right hand touched a piece of paper. She pulled it out, not remembering for a moment where it had come from. She studied it, wondering why she had taken it. It belonged in the drawer of Stella's desk. Again, at the back of her mind came a prickling of something that had to be remembered. What was it?

She tucked the paper under some T-shirts in her top dresser drawer.

The telephone rang, and Grannie shouted, "You get it. I've got these potatoes to finish. Somebody's got to do the kitchen work!"

Jennifer ran to the kitchen and picked up the telephone receiver after the third ring. "Hello?"

It sounded as though the voice were filtered through a thick cloth. "Watch out, little girl."

"What?" Jennifer's mind was a blank, cold hollow. "What?" she repeated, as thoughts refused to form.

The chuckle was so unexpected that Jennifer shivered. "Dead men tell no tales. Yo ho ho and a bottle of rum."

"Is this Elton?" But the voice was thick and soft. It didn't sound like Elton.

Jennifer took a long breath. Anger was chasing the fear from her mind. "What kind of a jerk are you?" she demanded. "All this dumb stuff isn't funny! Are you playing some kind of a joke?"

"No joke." The voice was a whisper now, even more frightening than before. "Back off, Jennifer," it said, "or else."

Can she be trusted? I'd been too hasty when I'd
... my... V... node...
least it was time... ... ... and I really
wanted to talk... ... ...
tie is and...

Funny thing... ... ...
stand for... ...
business.

Jennifer... ... ... may know what will
be next in line.

12

Can she be warned off? Will that get rid of her? It's worth a try. Yo ho ho and a bottle of rum. That was funny. At least it was funny to me. And it scared her. That's what I wanted to do—scare her good. Maybe she'll think a lunatic is after her. That's funny, too.

First Stella, then Darryl. What made him think I'd stand for blackmail? A punk like that cutting into my business!

Jennifer could be third. Better scare off, kid, or you'll be next in line.

13

"Who was that?" Grannie's head was cocked on one side. She looked as wary as a plump hen with a stranger in the henhouse.

Jennifer gripped her hands to keep them from trembling. She deliberately opened the cabinet over her head and, one by one, took down the plates to put on the table. "Just a prank call," she said. "Some kid, I guess."

"You seemed kind of upset for just a prank call. Look at you now, holdin' your back so funny and puttin' spoons on instead of forks."

By now Jennifer knew that whatever Lucas said, he meant. He couldn't find out about this call, or he wouldn't let her help. She wouldn't be able to stand being made to stay home like a protected little kid. Bobbie was her friend. She needed her.

"I'm so tired, Grannie. And all this about Bobbie—it's so hard." She whirled to face her grandmother. "Don't you understand?"

Grannie's face softened. "Look, why don't you put

your feet up and have a root beer or somethin' and rest awhile?" She sighed. "It's hard on my old feet, but it won't kill me to finish makin' supper by myself."

"I'll take care of it," Jennifer said. She reached into the refrigerator and pulled out a package of pork chops. "It will help if I can keep my mind busy with something else."

"If you say so." She had already begun edging toward the door. "I just might go in and listen to the TV news."

Jennifer quickly put the rest of the meal together. The breaded chops sizzled in their pan, splattering tiny drops of hot grease against the walls of the oven. She opened a can of sliced apples, dumping them into a saucepan with margarine and brown sugar and cinnamon, stirring them until the kitchen was warm with the spicy fragrance.

She knew about when to expect her father. His crew would work until daylight began to fade, then head back for the nursery. He'd carefully and slowly keep the day's records, go over the stock to be used the next day, check the tools, and on and on until he felt the job had been properly taken care of. As the days grew shorter, he'd have more time to rest in the evenings at home. So supper was ready to put on the table as soon as her father had washed up and taken his place at the head of the table.

Quickly, before Grannie had a chance to do so, Jennifer told her father about Lucas and his visit.

"It seems to me you're playin' at bein' the police," Grannie mumbled around a mouthful of potatoes.

"I don't understand why you can't leave it up to the police," Jennifer's father said.

In her intensity she leaned across the table toward him, gripping her hands together. "Dad, it's something I've got to do!"

"Well," he said. "Well, if you feel strongly about it, hon."

"I do," she said.

"All the time you're gonna waste you could be studying more or get a part-time job or whatever," Grannie said.

"No," Jennifer said.

Her father looked at Grannie and shrugged. "You—uh —met this policeman. He seemed all right to you?"

"He's not with the police now," Grannie said. "He's retired. Beats me why someone who's gettin' paid to stay home and go fishin' and whatever doesn't want to just do that. Believe me, if somebody paid me to—" She took another bite of potatoes, mashing her words with the food, so Jennifer didn't hear the rest of the sentence. It didn't matter. She knew what she had to do.

Soon after supper was over and the kitchen cleaned, Mark came.

"Come on out and sit on the steps with me," he said. "It's a pretty night, and there's hardly a mosquito around."

Jennifer sat on the steps, leaning into the support of Mark's arm. The air was heavy with sugar-sweetness from the honeysuckle on the fence and salt-sharpness from the bay. For a while neither of them spoke, until Jennifer let out a long sigh.

"Mrs. Trax's funeral is tomorrow."

"I know," Mark said. "You planning to go?"

"Yes. I have to."

"I thought you'd want to. That's one thing I came to tell you. I'll go with you."

"Thanks," she said. "I'll be awfully glad to have you there."

"Will they let Bobbie come? Do you know?"

"Oh, I hope they will! They have to! Mark, I want to see her so much!"

He nuzzled the top of her head with his chin. "I don't think they'll let you talk to her."

Jennifer sat upright and whirled to stare at him. "Why not?"

"Because she's in custody. Because when people are arrested they either let them out on bail or keep them away from other people. That's why."

She slumped against him. "It's not fair."

"If you keep wanting things to be fair, Jen, you're going to have a frustrating life."

Jennifer was silent for a few minutes, trying to decide what to do. Finally she said, "Mark, if Bobbie is there I'm going to do my best to try to talk to her."

"What will you say?" Mark asked.

"I don't know!" With a wail, Jennifer exploded into tears of tension against Mark's shoulder.

The funeral home was designed like a colonial plantation, and the small room to which Jennifer and Mark were directed was decorated with small Corinthian columns and a brightly hued stained-glass window that splashed garish colors across Estelle Trax's closed coffin. A small spray of flowers lay limply across the top of the coffin, and a wreath of tired purple chrysanthemums rested on a stand at one side.

As she stumbled into the back pew, pulling Mark with her, Jennifer noticed that they were the only young people in the room. Mrs. Aciddo sat near the front of the room. Her head tucked into her shoulders reminded Jennifer of a turtle peering out from the safety of its shell. Two women with bleached, teased, out-of-date hairstyles

huddled together in a middle pew. One of them cleared
her throat nervously and shot glances around the room as
though hoping for a quick rescue.

Bobbie wasn't there.

"They'll let her come, won't they?" she whispered to
Mark.

He shrugged, his broad shoulders straining the sports
coat he rarely wore and had outgrown. He made a face
and tugged at his collar and tie. "She's not a kid. She's
eighteen. They'd treat her like any other adult."

"But this is her mother!"

One of the blondes' flickering glances shot at Jennifer.
She glared at the woman and lowered her voice. "It's not
fair."

"You keep saying that. It doesn't change things."

A middle-aged, neatly dressed couple strolled in and
sat near the back. At the same time a slender man
dressed in a business suit entered the room at a side door
and fiddled with the microphone on the podium next to
the coffin, snapping it with his fingernail a couple of times
to test it.

Appearing satisfied, he gripped the edges of the podium and turned to the small congregation. The expres-
sion on his face slid into one of sympathy and compas-
sion. "Dear friends of the deceased," he began, but
stopped, his mouth slightly open, as Elton Krambo
strode into the room.

There was no mistaking that Elton and Darryl were
brothers. They scowled at the world from eyes that were
dark and shielded by secrets. Elton was taller and huskier
than Darryl, but their narrow features and unruly black
hair were almost identical.

Slowly, Elton walked down the aisle. He seemed to
pause for a moment as he stared at Jennifer, and she

shivered. He studied the others in the room, then took a seat in the front pew, motioning with a quick thrust of his hand for the minister to continue.

The man cleared his throat, then stammered quickly into a smooth recitation he must have given over and over again. "We—uh—come to pay our last respects to a dear mother—"

He nodded at Elton, who sat with arms tightly folded. Jennifer muttered, "She's *not* his mother," and Mark poked her into silence.

"—and good friend." On the minister went, but Jennifer tuned him out. Bobbie should be here. She had to talk to Bobbie. Maybe Lucas could work things out so that she could visit Bobbie in jail. She shivered again. When would this be over?

Mark pulled at her arm, and she realized that people were standing. The coffin was being wheeled through the side door. "Come on," he said. "We'll go to the cemetery."

In a few minutes Mark had steered his car into line, fourth and last behind the hearse and limousine. An officer on a motorcycle preceded them, holding traffic at the intersections as the procession drove through.

"I always wondered what it would be like to drive through all the red lights and have a cop—"

"Stop it!" Jennifer said.

"Hey, I know you feel bad, but don't take it out on me," Mark said.

"Sorry," Jennifer mumbled. "It's only that this is unreal. It's awful!"

"It's just one more thing to get through," Mark said. "You can do it."

The officer directed them into parking slots beside a shaggy lawn. They trooped over the grass, avoiding stepping on the tidy, rectangular grave markers and the round holes at each site, some of them filled with faded clumps of plastic flowers, most of them empty. They followed the coffin. It was carried by attendants to the side of a pit that had been camouflaged with a grass-green canvas.

Two brown metal folding chairs for family members had been set up at the side, but Elton avoided them and stood off, behind the others, who grouped into an uncomfortable, stiff semicircle, their faces glistening under the hot sun. The blondes murmured quietly to the middle-aged woman and the man with her. He ignored them, but she answered them.

A car came slowly down the road, nosing into an empty slot. Jennifer gasped as Bobbie and two police-women climbed out. Instinctively she stepped forward toward Bobbie, but Mark gripped her arm, stopping her.

The minister, who held an open prayer book in one hand, looked up at Jennifer and followed her gaze. He waited until Bobbie and the women with her had joined them, then began to read the prayers for the dead in a monotone.

A brightly colored van from one of the television stations pulled up with a screech of tires, and a cameraman hopped out. He hurried with his camera, tossing it to his shoulder, angling until he could see Bobbie's face, and zooming in with his special lens.

Bobbie didn't look at him. She didn't look at Jennifer, either. Her face was as expressionless as though she were asleep. She didn't seem to notice that the warm breeze was whipping strands of her yellow hair across her eyes and mouth. Jennifer wondered if this was Bobbie's defense—to let her mind escape even though her body couldn't.

The minister stopped speaking and turned to talk to one of the blond women who stood near him. Her lacquered hair moved only as she nervously nodded her head and began to edge away from him.

Jennifer pulled from Mark's grasp and ran toward Bobbie.

"Sorry," one of the policewomen said, and she held out a restraining hand. "Please don't come any closer."

Jennifer stopped. "Bobbie's my friend. I want to talk to her."

Bobbie looked up at Jennifer with dull eyes. "Hello, Jennifer," she said. "Thanks for coming."

"Bobbie, I've found someone who will help. Remember the man who came to see you—Lucas Maldonaldo? He believes in you, too."

The policewomen took Bobbie by the shoulders and turned her toward the road. Briskly, they walked with her to their car.

"Bobbie!" Jennifer cried. "We're going to find out who killed your mother! Bobbie! It's going to be all right!"

Mark came up behind her and gave her a quick shake. "Stop shouting," he grumbled. "Everybody's staring at you."

"They wouldn't let me talk to her." Jennifer rubbed the back of her arm across her eyes.

"Calm down. Your ex-cop friend didn't show."

"He wasn't sure that he could." She watched the police car drive off. Bobbie didn't even look back at her. "He told me to pay attention to who came to the funeral."

"Did you?"

"Well—yes." She watched the other cars leaving the cemetery road. "Elton was here, and Mrs. Aciddo, and those two blond women."

"And that couple who came in before Elton got here."

"Yes. That's it."

"So who were they?"

"What do you mean, who were—Oh, no! I should have found out."

"They've all gone. We're the last ones here, besides the guys over there at the grave site."

"I'm doing everything wrong. You're right. I should have got their names."

Mark shrugged. "You insisted on doing this. I think you should give up. You don't know the first thing about being a detective. It's just a waste of time, and you'll end up being more hurt than you are now." He took her hand. "My offer's still good. Padre Island would be beautiful this weekend."

"Don't think up excuses," she said. "They won't make it right." She walked toward Mark's car. "Will you drop me off at Chaparral?"

"What's at Chaparral?"

"The LaSalon beauty parlor."

"Since when have you started going to beauty parlors?"

"Since it occurred to me that those blond women probably work there. Maybe I can find out who they are and do something right for a change."

"You weren't paying attention to what I said. All the time I was talking you were thinking about those women."

"I heard you. Of course I did. But right now I've got a job to do."

"You act like you're a cop."

"Is that so bad?" Jennifer shrugged. "I suppose I could think of lots worse things than being a policewoman."

There was a small curl to Mark's lower lip, as though he wanted to pout, but he kept his voice matter-of-fact

and asked, "Don't you want to get some lunch and go
back to school?"

"Not now." Jennifer opened the car door and looked
up at Mark. "It's funny, but the hardest part of all of this
is doing all the same ordinary things that have to be
done, like going to school and eating meals and going to
bed at night and all the everyday things. Life keeps going
on when it ought to be frozen in place, so I can work on
what needs to be done for Bobbie."

As Mark stopped the car in front of LaSalon, Jennifer
stretched up to kiss him. The kiss landed at the corner of
his mouth, but Mark, his neck stiff with stubbornness,
did nothing to help correct it. Jennifer breathed in the
familiar warmth and sweat of his skin and for a moment
yearned to forget everything but being held in his arms,
but she straightened, shaking her thoughts back into
place, and said, "You were kind to come to the funeral
with me, Mark. You're a real friend."

It was the wrong word. She saw that she had hurt him
even more than before. She didn't know how to make it
right again, so she turned from the pain on his face, saying lightly, "I'll call you," and scrambled from the car.

It wasn't until she was directly in front of the door of
LaSalon that she noticed the small CLOSED card, with the
scrawled notation *Back at one.*

Jennifer's watch said twelve thirty, so she wandered
down to the corner, bought an egg salad sandwich to go
from a lunchroom drenched in the sizzle and smell of its
greasy griddle, and walked two blocks to Shoreline
Drive.

Gulls swooped at the bay, trying for a fish dinner, and
she watched the quiet water, a pale blue reflecting the

sunlight. She sat and yawned at the wavelets that gently flicked the seawall steps and felt her taut shoulders soften under the heat of the sun. She began to relax.

One ten. She broke the uneaten sandwich into pieces, tossing them to the gulls, who swarmed over and around her head. She left them to their greedy, screeching arguments, their frantic, flapping complaints, and walked briskly to LaSalon.

The CLOSED sign had vanished, and people were in the shop. She was so glad to see the pair of lacquered blondes, she smiled as though they were friends.

The nervous one was teasing a client's hair with trembling energy. She glanced up and down and up again at Jennifer with suspicion. The other woman sat behind a desk, slowly painting her fingernails.

"Do you have an appointment?" she drawled.

"No," Jennifer said. "I saw you at the funeral. Remember?"

The woman squinted to stare at her. "Oh," she said. "I thought you looked familiar when you came in. I guess you knew Stella."

"Yes." Jennifer kept herself from babbling too much. She was here to ask questions and get answers.

"Nice funeral," the woman added. "I guess you noticed those purple flowers. They came from the salon— from us."

"They were beautiful," Jennifer said, not remembering the flowers at all.

"We weren't too happy about them being purple, because Stella wasn't crazy about purple, but Margo here said she thought the purple looked kind of elegant."

She stopped and looked at Jennifer, waiting for her answer. "Oh, yes," Jennifer said, nodding enthusiastically. She didn't give the woman a chance to continue. "Are you the owner of LaSalon?"

The woman painted her thumbnail and held her hand close to her face, studying it critically. "Yeah."

"And you're—?"

"The owner, I said." She looked puzzled.

"I mean, what's your name?"

"Alice LaFleur," she said. "Really. I mean, it sounds so stagy and glamorous, but it's really my name. Margo tells me with a name like that I should have been a movie star."

Jennifer turned to Margo. "I'm Jennifer Lee Wilcox. You're Margo—?"

"Ouch!" Margo's customer cried as Margo teased with even more vigor.

"You're asking a lot of questions," Margo said. "How come?"

"Mrs. Trax's daughter is my best friend," Jennifer said. "I'm trying to get some information that might help her."

"We haven't got anything to tell you!"

"Oh, come on," Alice said. "It's a slow day. We haven't got anything else to do. We can answer a few questions."

"Thank you," Jennifer said.

Margo pressed her lips together tightly. When she didn't answer Jennifer's question, Alice giggled and said, "Margo's name is Smith. Now, everyone knows you can't be a movie star with a name like Smith."

"There's Roger Smith," Jennifer said.

"Huh? Well, I suppose, but he never got to be really, *really* famous."

"There was a couple at the funeral," Jennifer said.

"You talked with them. Could you tell me who they were?"

"Sure. She comes here regular on Thursdays. Mrs. Potter. She's nice but real fussy about her perms. She tips good, though."

"Did she know Stella?"

"Ouch!" Margo's customer complained. "What's got into you today, Margo? You're taking my scalp off!"

"It's nerves, honey," Alice explained. "Margo and I just got back from a funeral this morning, and I mean there is nothing harder than starting the day by going to a funeral."

"It was Stella Trax's funeral," Jennifer said.

The woman's eyes opened wide. "Oh, my gosh! I saw all about it on television. Murdered by her daughter!"

"No!" Jennifer cried. She willed herself to calm down and said, "I mean, some of us don't think Bobbie did it. We think it was someone else."

"Ouch! Will you quit pulling!" the woman shouted at Margo. "I respect your right to have a case of nerves, but you're killing me!"

"I'll be more careful," Margo mumbled. She poked with the end of a rattail comb into the raised mass of curls and waves she had created, patted and shaped a few stray hairs. Then she picked up a can of hair spray and shot a mist that enveloped her customer, causing Jennifer to cough and turn away.

It didn't seem to bother the woman. She gave herself a last, satisfied look in the mirror, discreetly placed a tip on the counter, and waited while Margo untied the plastic cape around her neck.

"Did you know Stella?" Jennifer asked the woman.

"My, no," the woman said. "I've only been coming

here twice a week for a month. She wasn't working here then."

"Comb-out on Fridays, wash and set on Tuesdays," Alice recited.

Jennifer waited until the woman had left. Margo disappeared somewhere into the back room of the shop, but Alice placidly began painting the nails on her right hand. "You wanted to know about Mrs. Potter," she said. "Sure, she knew Stella. She came to her ever since Stella started work here two years ago. She lives down the street from Stella, too."

"She has a son in high school?"

Alice examined a fingernail. "Yeah, she has a son. His name is Cody. I guess he's a good son, because we never heard much about him. Women talk about the problems in their families but not the others, unless it's about throwing a wedding or giving a big party or something like that. We usually hear about husbands."

Jennifer held on to the edge of the desk and asked in a rush, "Do you know anyone who might have murdered Mrs. Trax?"

Alice leaned forward to stare myopically into Jennifer's face. "How would I know anything about that?"

"I thought maybe you'd know if someone was threatening Mrs. Trax or frightening her."

"Nope. Her life was going okay, far as I could see. No real problems."

"Why did she quit her job here?"

Alice laughed. "Oh, honey, she didn't quit. I fired her. She was off more than she was on. Always calling in with some excuse. I mean, if she'd been sick or something I could understand that, but she felt fine. I think she just had something else going on that kept her so busy she didn't want to come to work."

"You mean like another job?"

"Maybe. It could have been another job. Or it could have been a man. We'll never know, will we?"

Jennifer sighed. "I'm trying to find out."

"Well," she said, "if it's any help, I'd bet it was a man in her life. If it was a job it would have to pay awfully good money—more money than Stella was worth, because Stella liked to shop. Oh, lordy, did Stella shop! Why, one of my customers came back from a trip to Houston, and what do you think? She ran right into Stella in one of those big shopping malls! No, I'm sure. It had to be a man, one with a fat wallet."

"Thanks for your help," Jennifer said. "If I have any more questions, could I come by again?"

"Sure," Alice said.

She went back to her fingernails, and Jennifer walked to the corner and sat on the bench at the bus stop. She took a spiral notebook out of her handbag and wrote down the names of the people at the funeral and everything she could remember that might be important.

She was aware that someone had sat at the end of the bench, but it wasn't until she stretched to tuck away her notebook and pencil that the person spoke. "What's in this for you?"

Jennifer jumped. "Elton!"

"Answer my question." His skin was the deep mottled red of someone with sunburn upon sunburn, the creases around his eyes and mouth making him look much older than his twenty-four years.

Jennifer wasn't afraid of Elton, but she was wary. She had talked to him on brief occasions when she was with Bobbie, but she didn't know him as well as she knew Darryl. He had always been reserved and quiet and had seemed to be a part of the adult world.

"I'm trying to help Bobbie," she said. "I don't believe that she murdered her mother. That's all I'm trying to do —help."

"Give it up," he said. "Don't get in the way."

Jennifer's back stiffened. "Is that a threat?"

"It's a warning," he said. He stood, and Jennifer scrambled to her feet, facing him.

"You don't scare me," she said.

"Too bad," he said. "You might wish I had." He turned abruptly, walked to an old, dented pickup truck parked in the middle of the block, and drove away.

A bus swooped down with a cloud of choking exhaust. Jennifer shook her head at the driver, who had opened the front door and was waiting for her, and walked quickly through the downtown area toward her home. This time when Lucas called, she'd have some positive news for him. But she couldn't wait for his call. She phoned his number four times, eager to reach him, wanting to tell him about Elton, and desperate to move ahead, to learn something else, but his telephone rang on and on and no one answered.

She was sitting at the kitchen table next to the telephone, trying to keep her mind on her English homework, when Lucas finally telephoned.

"I've got some information for you," she said, and she read off her notes about Margo and Alice in a rush.

"Very good," he said. There was a pause. "I don't hear you complaining that now there are only more questions to answer."

"I guess it's because I'm getting used to the way investigators work."

"Then you've finally made a start," he said.

"But I don't get used to you!" Jennifer said.

"Calm down. I'll go over my notes with you. I was at

the hospital this morning, then spent a while in Records, doing the nitty-gritty work."

"Hospital?" She interrupted him. "Oh—with Darryl."

"He's going to be in intensive care for a while, but the doctor's pretty sure Darryl will get over his beating."

"Did he tell you what happened to him?"

"Not a word. Darryl is scared pretty badly. It's my opinion whoever beat Darryl thought he'd killed him. We'll let him keep that thought. We admitted Darryl to the hospital under an assumed name."

"You think Darryl is trying to protect someone?"

"Do you know anyone he'd want to protect that much?"

"Elton," she said. "It could have been his brother, Elton." And she told him about Elton's conversation with her.

"Anything's possible." He paused. "Maybe you should take Elton's advice."

"No! I'm not afraid of Elton," she said in a rush of words. "He talked to me out in public where he could be seen, with traffic going by. If he were going to harm me he wouldn't do that, would he?"

"I'm giving that some fast consideration."

"Please, Lucas. Remember, we're working together. We're partners in this. I can help you solve this murder if you let me."

"Your safety is my primary concern. The case comes second."

"I'll be okay. Elton knows if anything happened to me he'd be suspect. Right?"

She waited, finding it hard to breathe, until Lucas answered. "You might be right. Just promise to tell me if he contacts you again."

"I promise." She changed the subject quickly before he

had second thoughts. "Can't you make Darryl tell you who did it?"

"How? By giving him another beating?"

"Don't get sarcastic," Jennifer said. "At least we know something. He told us that Stella wasn't his mother, so I guess she wasn't Elton's mother either."

"Or Bobbie's."

"What?"

"That's what I found out in Records today. Stella was not Bobbie Trax's mother."

14

Margie White with Newseye at Five. Today Estelle Trax was modestly and quietly buried at Rose Hill Memorial Park in Corpus Christi, with only a handful of friends in attendance. Although Lieutenant Darvy had informed the press that Bobbie Trax, arrested Tuesday for the murder of her mother, would not be allowed to be present at the funeral, at the last minute she was spirited from the county jail and brought, in the company of two police-women, to the cemetery. Without emotion, without displaying any signs of sorrow, Bobbie Trax was present to see the coffin containing her mother's body lowered into its grave. Newseye has brought you these exclusive films, which will be repeated during our newscast at ten o'clock tonight.

Both of them at the funeral. What a laugh. Especially the one who always makes me think of a wild-eyed cat with a dog on her tail. Thought she had to come, I guess.

That girl was there, too. Jennifer Wilcox. You don't know how close I'm watchin' you, do you Jennifer Wilcox? If you did, girl, you'd run.

Maybe she's making me edgy. Or maybe it's wondering about the stuff. It's got to be somewhere in the house. If the police had found it, we'd know.

Maybe I should go back and take a look.

Maybe tonight. Or maybe tomorrow night when I think this thing through and figure where she might have hid it.

Yeah. Maybe tomorrow.

15

"I don't understand," Jennifer said. "What makes you think that Mrs. Trax wasn't Bobbie's mother?"

"Records," Lucas said. "It's down in black and white. Bobbie Jane Simney was born in Memorial Hospital to a Dorothy Simney, no father listed."

"Bobbie Jane Simney doesn't even have the same name as Bobbie Trax! And why—?"

"Do you want to listen and learn something?"

"Okay. I'm sorry. It's just that what you said scares me. If Mrs. Trax isn't Bobbie's mother—then it looks worse for Bobbie, doesn't it?" Jennifer clamped her lips together and waited.

"Don't jump to unfounded conclusions," Lucas said. "Right now we're simply discussing facts. According to police records and old newspaper stories, when Bobbie was about two years old, her mother, Dorothy Simney, was killed in a knife fight in a bar. Dorothy's sister, Mrs. Stella Krambo, and her husband, Arthur Krambo, were given custody of the child."

"If they adopted her, then her name ought to be Krambo."

"They didn't adopt her. Soon afterward Stella and Arthur were divorced. By the time Bobbie was old enough to go to school, Stella had married Floyd Trax, and Bobbie was enrolled in school as Bobbie Trax. That marriage lasted only a few years, and Stella was divorced again."

"But Elton and Darryl lived with Stella, too. I wonder why, when none of the children were hers."

"I'm guessing, and it would take a lot of unnecessary research to find out. But I think we could say that since Stella's ex-husband Arthur was in the navy, he was probably away on sea duty a lot. His first wife, the mother of his sons, died when they were very young. He could have sent an allotment to Stella to take care of the boys."

Jennifer let out a long sigh. "You found out so much just by hunting through old records."

"Still got the movie idea of what a private eye does? You'll find out it's mostly a lot of legwork, a lot of sitting in chairs going through old newspaper clippings and city and county and police records."

Jennifer thought of the threatening telephone call she had received and gave a sharp laugh. "Yeah, boring stuff," she said.

There was a pause. "Something wrong?"

"No," Jennifer said quickly. "I was just thinking. Do we find out where those husbands are? They could be suspects."

"Arthur lives in Arizona, mostly on disability pay from the navy. Floyd died a few years ago."

"That puts us back with a lot of questions and no answers. Could we look in Mrs. Trax's handbag? Maybe that would give us some clues. She carried this large bag, and it always seemed to be stuffed."

"No handbag on the property list," Lucas said. "If there had been a handbag, the police would have taken possession of it, and we would have no legal right to go through it." He paused. "You know, a missing handbag was one of the reasons I decided to take this case. If Bobbie had taken money from Stella's bag when she ran away, the bag would have been somewhere in the house. If she'd taken the bag itself, it would have been in that lean-to on the beach. But since a handbag seems to be nonexistent, I've felt from the beginning there was someone else involved."

"But I—" Jennifer stopped herself in time, her heart thumping in her ears. "That is," she amended, "you're saying that even if the police had the handbag, we couldn't look through it."

"Right."

"So what do we do next?" Jennifer knew what she was going to do, but she wasn't going to tell Lucas. If he was aware of what she knew—that there was a loose board in the floor of one of the kitchen cabinets where Mrs. Trax always hid her handbag—he'd be honor bound to tell the detective working on the case. Jennifer didn't feel honor bound to anyone but Bobbie.

"For the moment you don't have to do anything," Lucas was telling her. "Tomorrow I've got some more work to do in Records, and I'm going to try to talk to Bobbie."

"Could I go with you?"

"Not this time. Not yet."

"She's my friend. I want to see her."

"You hired me, Jennifer. Now let me call the shots."

"Okay," Jennifer said. "Is it all right with you if I go to see Mrs. Trax's neighbor? That Mrs. Potter?"

"I think it would be a good idea. I'll be in touch."

"Good-bye, Lucas," Jennifer said. Her fingers were

trembling as she hung up the telephone. She would talk to Mrs. Potter, but first she was going to the Trax house to find that handbag.

"I forgot to tell you—" Grannie spoke behind her, and Jennifer jumped. "Good heavens, girl! You're spooked today. All I said was—"

"I'm sorry, Grannie. I didn't hear you come in the kitchen."

"Well, I was goin' to tell you, if you don't keep interruptin', that Roy's goin' to pick up some fried chicken and stuff for our dinner, so you don't have to fix nothin'." She sighed. "Only he's goin' to be a mite late. Probably goin' to have a drink with that woman before he heads for home."

"With Gloria," Jennifer said automatically. "Grannie, it's Friday. Dad needs to relax. Saturday is one of his busiest days at the nursery."

"I give him credit for bein' a good, hard worker," she said. "It's just that I don't know why he wants to waste his time on that woman."

Jennifer patted her grandmother's shoulder. "I'm going out for a little while. I'll be back pretty soon—probably before Dad gets home. Look—I'll set the table right now, so everything will be ready, and you can watch your television programs."

"It's late," Grannie complained. "The news is over." She brightened. "Say, they showed the funeral on TV. I looked for you, but they just showed Bobbie and the coffin and not you or the other people there."

Jennifer shuddered. "I won't be long, Grannie." She left before her grandmother could offer any more objections.

It didn't take long to get to Bobbie's house. It was dark by the time she arrived, and she was glad. If that nosy

Mrs. Aciddo saw her, she might get in trouble. She hadn't brought a flashlight because she knew where Mrs. Trax kept one—in the left-hand drawer in the kitchen.

She had come into the yard from the street behind Bobbie's, a shortcut they had used often, crossing a vacant lot and ducking through the oleander hedge. The cloying sweetness of the thick clusters of oleander blossoms made it hard to breathe, and the branches plucked at her shirt. For a moment Jennifer paused, looking around the yard, straining to see if there was any movement at Mrs. Aciddo's side windows, but they were dull with the darkness of an empty house.

Jennifer ran across the backyard and crouched under the window with the broken lock. Again she waited and watched. Again there was nothing but silence.

Slowly she got to her feet, pushed up the bottom section of the window, and hoisted herself to the sill. She was shaking as she climbed through the window and onto the sofa into a darkness so terrifying it was like a scream waiting to happen.

It crept over her—a feeling that the hovering shapes that began to emerge from the blackness were living and breathing and waiting for her to move so they could pounce. Was that the sound of her own breathing she heard? Or was someone else here with her, close enough to touch?

Jennifer wanted to panic, to run, to dive through the window, but she clutched the edge of the sofa cushion and waited until her eyes became adjusted to the darkness. Of course she was alone, she told herself. She had given in to panic, that's all. She took a few steady, long breaths, willing herself to calm down, to do the job she had come here to do.

Finally she was able to get to her feet and make her way past the massive armchair to the kitchen.

The flashlight first. She opened the drawer, and her groping fingers immediately closed on the cold metal shaft of the flashlight. Quickly she turned it on, aiming it at the floor.

Jennifer didn't know if she felt better with or without the pencil-slim shaft of light. It seemed to make the shadows larger, the dark of the living room more ominous. She stooped and opened the last cabinet on the left, lifting up the board that covered the bottom.

There lay the handbag.

Jennifer pulled it out, replacing the board without a sound, as though trying to shield her actions from that listening house.

She sat on the floor, the bag on her lap, and opened it. There was a small vinyl case that bulged tightly against the snap that held it shut. Jennifer opened it first. Inside were credit cards and carbons from credit card purchases. She was about to close it, puzzled why Mrs. Trax had so many cards and would save the carbons, when she noticed the name on one of the cards. It wasn't Stella Trax. She thumbed through the other cards. They were made out in a variety of names. The carbons, too. Most of those came from a small jewelry store, although a few were from a drugstore. Jennifer was familiar with both the stores. They were in a shopping strip in the south part of Corpus Christi. It dawned on her that the credit cards had probably been stolen, but what would Mrs. Trax be doing with those carbons?

In the zippered side pockets of the bag were a wad of tissues, a couple of lipsticks and a comb, a pair of dark glasses, some bankbooks and a checkbook held together with a rubber band, a candy bar, and a small note pad with a stub of a pencil attached. On the pad was a telephone number. Not a name, just a number. But Jennifer didn't need the name to know whose phone number she was staring at.

Lucas Maldonaldo's.

Why would Mrs. Trax have Lucas's phone number in her handbag? She must know him. How? And why didn't he say something about knowing Stella? Was he keeping something from her?

Jennifer snapped the handbag shut and jumped to her feet, slamming the cabinet door. Lucas and his unbending, patronizing ways! Lucas, who thought she had so much to learn! She had learned that Lucas hadn't been honest with her. She was going to face him with this and demand an answer!

When she arrived at his house, Stella's handbag tucked firmly under her arm, Jennifer didn't just ring the bell, she pounded on the door. She could hear his quick, firm footsteps, and the door flew open. His eyes widened when he saw her.

"You knew Stella Trax and you didn't tell me!" she said.

Lucas shook his head wearily and moved to one side. "Come on in," he said. "Let's find out what's on your mind."

He lowered himself into what was obviously his favorite armchair from the way the faded lumps and bumps seemed to fit around him. "Sit down," he said.

"I don't want to sit down."

"Sit down," he repeated. "Then we'll talk."

Jennifer perched on the edge of the sofa, facing him. She held out the handbag. "This belonged to Mrs. Trax."

"What are you doing with it?" He leaned forward.

"I knew where she hid her handbag. One night, when I slept over at Bobbie's, I got up to go to the bathroom, and I saw Mrs. Trax put her handbag in what must have been her special hiding place in the kitchen. Mrs. Trax didn't see me, and I didn't say anything, but I remembered."

"Why didn't you tell me?"

"I've never told anyone, not even Bobbie. I guess I was afraid to. She had told me that her mother kept the hiding place a secret from everyone, even her kids. Darryl was always after her for money, and I don't think she trusted any of them."

Lucas rubbed his shoulder. "Taking that handbag was a stupid thing for you to do."

"Don't you dare get mad at me when I'm so mad at you! I'm the one who has a right to be angry!"

He leaned back in his chair. "Anger will only get in our way. Tell me what's bothering you, and then I'll read you out for taking something that doesn't belong to you."

"I looked through this handbag without telling you, because you said it would be the property of the police, and if they had it we couldn't see what was in it. I'll show you what I found and you can be upset with me if you want to, but you'll have some explaining to do to the police in any case."

"You haven't made sense about what you want from me."

"I want an answer. Finally I've got a question that has to have an answer right away." She pulled the little note pad from Stella's handbag and tossed it to him. "What was Mrs. Trax doing with your telephone number?"

Lucas stared at it and looked up at Jennifer. "I have no idea."

"Are you going to tell me you didn't know her?"

"In a roundabout way I knew her," he said. "I was the investigating officer on the case concerning her son Elton. I'm the one responsible for his being sent to prison on a robbery conviction."

"Oh," Jennifer said. She leaned back against the puffy sofa, her anger disappearing as fast as hot air from a split balloon. "You didn't tell me that. I didn't know."

"It looks as though she wanted to talk to me about something," he said.

"But she didn't?"

"She didn't."

Jennifer shook her head. "Then we don't know why she had written your phone number on her note pad. And it doesn't clear up my questions about the credit cards."

"What credit cards?"

Jennifer got up and took him the handbag. She walked back to the sofa and plopped on it. "Inside that bag are a wad of credit cards with other people's names on them."

Lucas opened the bag and methodically went through it. She could practically see a computer behind his eyes as he neatly catalogued every item he saw. While he studied the contents of the vinyl folder, Jennifer ran a finger across the coffee table.

"You never dust, do you?" she said.

He didn't answer.

"And you don't put anything away. All those old magazines stacked on the floor, and two dirty coffee cups, and that bottle of aspirin." She felt a little sorry for him, because obviously he'd been used to his wife doing all those things for him, but for some reason she also felt like needling him. "You ought to get someone to clean this place for you once in a while, if you're not going to do it yourself."

He glanced at her for only a second, but his eyes were as vulnerable as a child's. For an instant he was no longer a tough cop, but someone who was hurting badly.

Jennifer, guilt hunching her shoulders, said, "Tell me about your wife. What was she like?"

He shrugged. "She was a gentle person. Patient with me. Patient with the long, irregular working hours an officer has to keep when he's on a case."

"I guess it must be hard being married to a cop."

"Lila never complained." He looked around the room. "She knew how to keep the house up. I still haven't learned."

"Maybe you don't want to." He frowned, and she added, "I mean, I was like that with chemistry. I didn't like it, so I didn't care if I learned it or not." She paused. "In case you're wondering, I did pass it."

"That's the least of my worries," he said, one corner of his mouth turning down in a familiar way that made Jennifer feel comfortable again. "You know what these are?" He held up a handful of credit cards. "A couple of these cards look like the real thing, probably stolen, but most of them seem to be counterfeit cards. Look at this one—the bad printing at the bottom."

"You mean they're just made-up names and numbers?"

"Nope. The names and numbers are real. The whole scam is right here in front of us. Apparently, Stella was able to get hold of some carbons from actual sales. Merchants throw them out in the trash, and many commercial trash bins are open to scavengers. Someone steals a wad of carbons, and from these carbons names and numbers are taken to be used on fake cards. Then shoppers use the cards, and the charges are simply put on the bills of the innocent victims."

"I thought store clerks called in to check on the sales."

"Only if the sales are over a certain amount—usually fifty dollars. So the thief spends a lot of time buying items that cost less, like small appliances, silver bowls, clothing. There are a lot of things that you can get for under fifty dollars."

"What would Mrs. Trax do with stuff like that?"

"I doubt if she kept any of it. The stolen stuff is fenced."

Jennifer studied Lucas. "You seem to know a lot about this credit card thing."

"You bet I do," he answered. "Remember—I'm a police officer, and this credit card scam has been going on for a long time all over the United States. It's hard to catch the people involved in it, but we do know that a clever thief can charge at least five thousand dollars' worth of items in a day's work."

"So that's why Stella shopped so much." She remembered something. "And the woman in the beauty salon said Stella even went out of town to shop."

"And to steal a few cards and carbons, no doubt." Lucas slowly got to his feet. He stood and rubbed his lower back. "You realize that now we have an entirely different set of circumstances, which may or may not lead to another motive for Stella's murder by someone other than Bobbie."

Jennifer jumped up. "So they might let Bobbie go?"

"No. Circumstantial evidence is still strongly against her. But this means another lead, another direction. If Stella was involved in a stolen and counterfeit credit card ring, then someone in that ring might have been responsible for her death."

"Why would someone want to kill her?"

"Maybe she was getting greedy. Maybe she wanted a bigger cut."

"Or maybe," Jennifer said, "she wanted to tell you about it. She knew who you were because of Elton's arrest. Maybe she was going to phone you and didn't get the chance."

"Could be."

Lucas walked toward the phone. "I'll call in. Tell them about the handbag."

"What about that pad with your telephone number? Shouldn't we—?"

He scowled at her. "Trying to protect me now, are you?"

"I didn't want you to get in trouble."

"You've got so much to learn, Jennifer. That number might fit into the puzzle and help solve this crime. In any case, it wouldn't be honest to remove it."

"I was just trying to help."

"Then work by the rules."

"Should I take the handbag back to the house?"

"No." He picked up the receiver. "But you'd better stick around for a while."

"So you can 'read me out,' as you said? You haven't done that yet."

One corner of his mouth twisted into the semblance of a smile. "I've decided not to. You'll get enough of that from Detective Carl Robbins."

Detective Robbins was built something like a bear. Jennifer was sure he had probably played football in school. His hair was thick and sandy and hung in his eyes. Dog or cat hair clung to his rumpled slacks. His partner,

Detective Arturo Casals, was small and neat with a tiny black mustache that looked as though it had been drawn on his face. He scowled at Jennifer and let Detective Robbins do the talking.

And talk he did, finishing with "So what you did was not only stupid and dangerous but illegal."

"I was trying to help my friend," Jennifer said.

He turned to Lucas, who was leaning back in his armchair, as relaxed as though they'd been having a conversation about baseball scores. "What did this kid get you into, Lucas?"

"Jennifer didn't get me into anything," Lucas said calmly. "She came to me for help. After I studied the case I decided to take it, and I invited Jennifer to be my partner." For a moment Jennifer thought he'd actually smile at her, but he sat upright and, in a tone of voice as firm as his backbone, said, "Carl, she needed some cutting down to size, and you did a good job of it, but you can lay off now."

Carl frowned. "Trespassing, interfering with police procedure, removing property . . . I don't know."

"Well, I do," Lucas said. "She's given you some solid evidence in that credit card scam. Let's just go on from there." He gestured toward the pad of paper with his telephone number written on it. "It's just a hunch, but I think Stella Trax was planning to contact me regarding the scam."

"Could be," Carl said.

"We'll never know, will we?" Art added. "And our next question is: Who else in this town besides Stella Trax is working the racket?"

"Mrs. Aciddo," Jennifer said.

The three men looked at her. "What else do you know that you haven't told us?" Carl asked.

Jennifer shook her head. "I don't know it. I just think so, because she told the reporters that she and Mrs. Trax had planned to go shopping."

Art shrugged. "Lots of women go shopping together."

Jennifer insisted. "But she lied about Mrs. Trax's job at the beauty salon. She said she still worked there, only she didn't."

"Maybe Stella hadn't told her she'd quit."

"You could follow her and find out."

"On just your hunch?" Art shook his head. "Without any solid information about Mrs. Aciddo, we can't spend the man-hours on tailing her.

"We'll share this with the FBI people working the scam," Art said.

"The FBI is in this too?" Jennifer was puzzled.

"It's an interstate crime," Carl said. "A regular syndicate that uses credit cards to rob nationally—even internationally."

"You found the handbag," Lucas said. "That's all the information the FBI needs. Right?"

Carl studied Jennifer for a long moment, then mumbled, "She couldn't help them." He lumbered to his feet and picked up the handbag. "We'll be in touch," he said to Lucas. He pointed a finger at Jennifer, so close that it almost brushed her nose. "Kid," he said, "keep clean, do just what Lucas tells you to do and nothing more. And don't mention any of this about the credit cards to *anyone*. Understand? The last thing we'd need would be for word to get out on the streets or for the media to know."

Jennifer nodded, not trusting herself to answer. If they weren't interested in finding out if Mrs. Aciddo fit into the credit card scheme, it didn't matter. She didn't need their help. She knew what to do. She'd follow Mrs. Aciddo and see what she could find out.

16

I've got to go back for another look. It's the only way to get rid of this damn headache. I know why the headache won't go away. It's not because of Stella. It's because of her handbag.

Yeah, I remember that big handbag she always carried with her. Wouldn't let it out of her sight. And hid it when she wasn't carrying it. Never trusted anyone, even the kids. Especially the kids. Especially Darryl, who nearly went crazy looking for it when she wouldn't give him money for a fix. That's where the stuff has to be. She'd have cards in it. Sure she would. She was holding out.

Dumb Stella. Dumb to hold out and try to cut your own deal. Didn't you know I'd find out?

I guess you weren't too dumb, were you? You had enough sense to hide the stuff. If the police got hold of it, the news would have been out. So it must still be there.

Now I know for sure. I'm going to the house to look for it.

17

The detectives drove Jennifer home. Lucas asked them to. In a way he told them to, because he didn't want her going home on the bus and walking from the bus stop. They had a lot of respect for Lucas. Jennifer could see that. She could also see that they were wondering if Lucas was temporarily out of his head to be working with her on a case they thought was a closed issue.

She opened the back door of their unmarked car as it pulled up in front of her house and jumped out the instant it stopped. "Thanks," she called to them, and ran up the walk to the front steps. Among the shadows she had seen the familiar broad-shouldered, hunched-over form of Mark. He was sitting on the top step, waiting for her.

As he saw Jennifer, he clambered to his feet and came toward her. "Jen," he said, "are you okay? I was worried."

Suddenly she was exhausted and longed for Mark

more than she ever had before. She hurried into his arms, holding him as though he were an anchor against the gale, and she were a small sailboat, skittering the tops of waves, in danger of flying out to sea.

His chin tucked her forehead against his chest, where she nuzzled his neck, the salty taste of his skin on her lips.

"Who were those guys?" he asked.

"Some detectives Lucas knows. Let's not talk about them."

"What were you doing in their car?"

"He asked them to give me a ride home."

"It's late, Jen. It's a little after eight."

Jennifer stepped back. "Darn you, Mark. I said I don't want to talk about those men or Bobbie or anything else. I just need you to hold me."

She could see the struggle as he wanted to pursue the questions, and was thankful when he began to relax. "Okay," he said, taking her hand and leading her toward the porch steps. "Sit down with me awhile. I wanted to—well, try to make things right with us again."

The breeze from the sea was cool, and Jennifer shivered. Mark put an arm around her shoulders, pulling her close. "I'm sorry," he said.

For a moment she couldn't remember. "For what?"

"For this afternoon. For when I got mad and drove off."

"Oh," Jennifer said. "I—Oh, that's all right, Mark."

"You didn't remember, did you?"

"Well, not at first. I mean, I hadn't been thinking about it, and—"

"Maybe you just didn't care."

"Of course I care!" Jennifer wrapped her arms around him tightly. "Oh, Mark, I've had so much to think about.

But that doesn't mean I don't care about you. You don't know how glad I was to see you when I came home a few minutes ago! I missed you! I needed to be with you!"

She lifted her face and kissed him hard before he could answer.

Finally he took her chin in one hand, tilting her head. The night darkened his hazel eyes, and they looked as deep and liquid as the midnight sea waters that lapped the piers of the T-heads. "Jennifer," he said, "I've been thinking a lot about you and me. This thing with Bobbie has got between us, but I can see how you feel about trying to do your best for her. So that part's okay. It's the other part, the part about maybe my pushing you to do something you don't want to do. I don't understand if it's that you just don't love me enough, or don't care enough, or what your reason is. And I think that hurt us, and I didn't mean to hurt us."

Jennifer leaned back and sighed. "You don't understand, do you?"

"I said I didn't."

"Okay, then, I'll tell you. I like to feel that I'm in charge of myself, that I'm important—at least to myself."

"You're important to me."

"Don't interrupt." She lightly pressed a finger against his lips. "I'm trying to tell you that part of feeling good about myself is to not go to bed with you or anybody else until I'm ready. And I've decided that's going to be after I'm married."

"Kind of old-fashioned, aren't you?"

"Nope. It's just part of wanting to like myself. It's not an old idea. It's not a new idea. It's just an idea I feel comfortable with."

Mark was silent for a few minutes. Then he said, "I'll wait. If that's what you want, Jen, I can wait."

Jennifer couldn't help giggling. "You sound as pompous as an old preacher!"

Mark had to laugh, too. "You think *I* sound pompous? How about you? Anyhow, I only meant—"

"I know what you meant, and I'm glad we talked about it."

She felt light and giddy and giggled again. Snuggled against Mark, she lifted her face for another kiss, but the door behind them suddenly opened and light from the living room spilled over them. "So there you are!" Grannie's voice was shrill. "That leftover chicken's cold enough to be laid out and buried! Where have you been, Jennifer Lee Wilcox?"

Jennifer and Mark scrambled to their feet in a tangle of legs, bumping knees, and elbows.

"I'm sorry, Grannie," Jennifer said. "I've been here talking with Mark."

"Least you could of done was come inside long enough to tell me you was home. Your father may not know which side is up with that woman here and her mouth runnin' on and on, but I've been sittin' in the kitchen, watchin' the clock and frettin'."

"I'll come in now," Jennifer said. She tugged at Mark's hand. "I'm hungry," she told him. "I'll race you to the cold chicken."

"Speak your piece to your father and that woman first." Grannie snorted. "Remember you got manners."

Jennifer led the way into the living room. Her father and Gloria, who looked as though they'd been jammed together at one end of the sofa, glowed like kids at a birthday party at the moment the presents are opened. Her father's browned cheeks were touched with pink, and his eyes sparkled. She loved seeing him so happy. For so many years his life had seemed quiet and dull, and she had felt sorry for him without knowing what to do to help him.

"Well, hon," he said, "Gloria and I have been wondering when you'd get here."

Jennifer bent to kiss him and smiled. "You don't look as though you've missed me."

Gloria giggled, and her fingers fluttered around her chin, playing with the large plaid velvet bow on the ribbon tied around the neck of her blouse.

"Sit down," Roy said. He gestured toward the chairs. "You too, Mama."

"I'd better go. This looks like family stuff," Mark said as Grannie grumblingly lowered herself into the straight chair near the door.

"Don't go. Have a seat, Mark. You're practically family." Roy's beaming smile swept their faces, then shone on Gloria. "Gloria's going to be family, too."

"I seen it comin'," Grannie mumbled as Mark offered congratulations and Jennifer hurried to hug Gloria.

"You don't mind?" Gloria was suddenly shy as she clung to Jennifer's hand. "I know how kids sometimes feel about stepmothers, and I wouldn't want you to feel like that about me."

"I'm not a kid, Gloria," Jennifer said. "I'm glad that you can make Dad so happy."

"That's a nice thing to say, hon." Roy reached over to squeeze her other hand. "You're a good girl."

Grannie gave a long sigh. "I suppose I better start lookin' for another place to live."

"Mama," Roy said, "you've got no call to think like that. You and Gloria will get along fine."

Gloria's smile began to freeze at the edges, and Roy looked like someone whose shoes pinched his feet.

"Grannie," Jennifer said quickly, "right now all we

want to think about is celebrating with Dad and Gloria. We ought to have some champagne and caviar!"

"Champagne?" Grannie snorted. "All we got around here is root beer and crackers!"

Jennifer's laughter shot through the room like a fireball, igniting even her grandmother. "Then let's bring out the root beer and crackers! Tonight we're going to party!"

Saturday morning Jennifer awoke early, the sun prodding her eyelids like an animated alarm clock. For a few moments she stretched, poking at the puzzling guilt feeling in the back of her mind, until it bobbed to the surface and became something to face.

"I didn't forget about you, Bobbie," she murmured aloud. "Well, I did forget for a little while, but it was something special. It was Dad's night, and—"

She sat up, kicking off the blanket and sheet, swinging her legs over the side of the bed, and jamming her feet into her sandals. "Darn! I'm talking to myself!"

The problem with life, she thought as she ate a quick breakfast of cereal and toast washed down with orange juice, was that it came in so many parts, and sometimes those parts overlapped. Last night it was Dad's turn, but now she had to get back to work to help Bobbie. And somehow she had to do something about Grannie. Dad wouldn't know how to handle things. And there was school. She'd have to get back to classes, or she'd have problems at exam time.

And Mark.

Last night she had loved being with Mark. Today she didn't even want to think about him. Each day she was one day closer to graduation and the day Mark expected her to marry him. But—

She swept her dishes under the hot-water faucet to rinse them, then stacked them on the counter near the sink. No time to think about other things. She had to keep her mind on the next step in helping Bobbie. If she could only talk to her.

Why not? Surely people in jail could have visitors. Lucas had gone to see Bobbie. If he had, then why couldn't she visit Bobbie, too! As her excitement grew, she doubled her efforts to be quiet. Her father was already at work at the nursery, but Grannie was asleep. If she could get out of the house before Grannie woke up, it would make what she wanted to do a lot easier.

The new courthouse building rose over Waco Street and Mestina. Gleaming white, in a modular design, it seemed too elegant to stand face-to-face with Luckie's Bail Bonds and the cramped old buildings that crowded around it. The interior, built around an atrium lobby with trees, a statue of a soaring seagull, and gleaming escalators, confused Jennifer. There were discreet signs on the grass-cloth walls directing visitors to courtrooms and offices of justices of the peace down brown-and-white-carpeted hallways, but she could find nothing that informed visitors that a jail existed in this shining place.

She became aware that a uniformed guard stood near one hallway, so she asked him for help.

"Sure," he said. "You don't just go to the jail. That's over in the old section of the building facing Waco Street. So's the sheriff's office. You go down this hall to get there, and they'll give you all the information you need to visit somebody and what days and times you can go."

"I didn't think about special visiting hours."

"You're too early, you know."

"No. I didn't know."

"Well, go ask them the procedure." He pointed in the

direction of the office, and it didn't take her long to find it.

There were a few people with briefcases in the office. A woman and man were talking to each other. Another man, a very young man with black curly hair, was talking to a woman at a desk.

"I should be with Miss Trax less than half an hour," he was saying as he clipped a large plastic badge to his right lapel.

"Miss Trax? Bobbie?" Jennifer cried.

Everyone stopped and stared at her. Her face grew hot, and she stammered, "I'm sorry." She hurried to the side of the man at the desk, glad that the couple had resumed their conversation. "I'm Jennifer Wilcox," she said. "I'm Bobbie Trax's best friend. I want to see her, too."

He studied her a minute, then stuck out his right hand. "I'm Richard Purtry, Miss Trax's attorney. I'm afraid you've come at the wrong time. Visiting hours are from twelve to two thirty today and tomorrow."

"I'll come back," Jennifer said quickly. She realized she had grabbed his arm, and she pulled her hands back, holding them together. "I'm sorry. It's just that I need to talk to her. I need to see her. Is she all right? How does she feel?"

"She's all right," he said. He looked at his watch. "If you've got a few minutes, we'll see if we can find a couple of chairs in an empty room. I'd like to ask you a few questions."

Jennifer nodded eagerly. "Sure. Anything." She followed him down the hallway, through an open door, and sat where he indicated. He sat next to her, took out a note pad and shiny silver pen, adjusted the pad on his lap, fiddled with the tip of the pen, then turned to face her. She was amazed that he didn't look much older than some of the guys in school. He had round cheeks in a round face and skin as light and smooth as a cosmetics ad.

"Are you really old enough to be a lawyer?" Jennifer blurted out.

He scowled and sighed. "I take after my mother's side of the family. Nobody looks older than kindergarten. It's not my fault."

"Maybe you should grow a mustache."

"I did. It looked silly."

"Maybe you should look silly instead of young. Are you right out of law school?"

"It doesn't matter." He ruffled the pad of paper and cleared his throat. "Now—a couple of questions."

"It matters to me," Jennifer interrupted. "Do you know Lucas Maldonaldo?"

"No."

"Well, Lucas and I are trying to find out who really killed Mrs. Trax. If we can't make it, then it's up to you to save Bobbie."

"My job is not to save people. My job is to defend their constitutional rights."

"You're supposed to get her out. You want to be a good lawyer, don't you, and win all your cases?"

"Even the best lawyers don't win all their cases."

"You wouldn't have taken this case if you didn't believe in Bobbie's innocence, so—"

It was Purtry's turn to interrupt. "I didn't take this case because I believed in your friend. I took it because it was assigned to me. I don't defend criminals. I defend their constitutional rights."

Jennifer leaned back and stared at him. "You think she's guilty!"

"I'm trying to find out as much as I can. And your

friend Bobbie isn't being very helpful. She just keeps telling me the same story over and over, about how she
quarreled with her mother and ran away to Padre Island."

"She tells you the same story because it's the truth!"

He brought the tip of his pen to the paper. "You can
verify this?"

"I—uh—it's just that she told me. I know. I'm the one
who found her and told her about her mother, and she
hadn't known! I'm sure of it!"

He wrote a few words on the paper. "We may ask for
your testimony," he said, "but it's not enough to con-
vince a jury."

"Or you?"

"Let me ask you a few questions." He looked at his
watch again. "We'll make it quick. First of all, give me
your full name, address, and telephone number."

A few minutes later he ushered Jennifer out of the
room, shook her hand perfunctorily, and hurried down
the hallway. Jennifer fought back tears that pushed and
hurt behind her eyes. She wouldn't cry. She had other
things to do, and at twelve she'd be back here to see
Bobbie.

The sun warmed her shoulders as she waited for the
bus on Leopard Street. It wouldn't take long to get to
Bobbie's neighborhood and Mrs. Aciddo.

But as she left the second bus and walked down the
street toward Bobbie's house, she saw the boy who had
talked to her at school. He was standing in his front yard
with the woman who had been at the funeral with her
husband. She had on a pair of gardening gloves and kept
trying with the back of one arm to push away a damp
strand of hair that had fallen in front of her eyes. His blue
T-shirt was dark with sweat, and he held a bamboo rake

against one shoulder. Mrs. Aciddo's green sedan was parked in front of her house, which meant she was still home. Jennifer had wanted to talk to Mrs. Potter. Now seemed like a good time.

The mother and son stopped talking and watched her as she approached. The air was pungent with the musty fragrance of newly turned earth and the dry dustiness of shriveled brown leaves. "Hi," she said. "I'm Jennifer Wilcox." She turned to Cody. "I apologize for being such a jerk when you tried to be nice to me. I was so upset I didn't know what to say or do. I shouldn't have taken it out on you."

His shoulders relaxed and he let out a long breath. "Hey, it wasn't your fault. I knew that." He turned to his mother. "Mom, Jennifer is Bobbie Trax's friend."

Mrs. Potter's eyes grew as wide and round as small doughnuts. "Oh, my," she said. "How sad."

"Mrs. Potter, I don't believe that Bobbie killed Mrs. Trax," Jennifer said.

"I hope you're right," she said. "Well, if you young people will excuse me, I'm going to try to get this yard in shape before lunch."

"It's you I need to talk to," Jennifer said. "It's about Mrs. Trax." She pulled her notebook from the left hip pocket of her jeans.

Mrs. Potter paused, again looking surprised. "I didn't know her very well, even though we were neighbors and all. I did go to her to get my hair done for a while."

"At LaSalon."

"Yes, but it didn't work out. Often she didn't come in on the day I had an appointment, and either Alice or Margo had to take me. Alice is all right—not as good as Stella was, but nothing to really complain about. But that Margo doesn't know what to do with your hair unless you bring her a picture, and even then she's not good at copying a hairstyle."

"Maybe she has trouble because she's so nervous."

"Margo? Nervous? Not that I'd noticed. I thought she was kind of dull, if anything."

"Did Mrs. Trax go in and out of her house a lot?"

Mrs. Potter shook her head. "I work during the week. I'm a bookkeeper at Dillard's Department Store. And when I'm home I'm so busy I don't have time to notice what the neighbors are up to. That's why Stella and I didn't do much in the way of neighboring."

"Can you think of anything you'd like to tell me about Mrs. Trax?"

Mrs. Potter thought a moment. Then she said, "Nothing. And I don't know how anything I told you could help Bobbie Trax."

"It's like pieces in a puzzle," Jennifer told her, aware that she was paraphrasing Lucas. "All the bits of information add up."

"Well," Mrs. Potter said, "I hope you'll come up with the right answers."

"Thanks," Jennifer said. She made a few notations in the notebook and shoved it and the pencil back into her pocket. "See you at school, Cody," she added, and walked back toward the bus stop.

Mrs. Potter and Cody were still working in the front yard. She couldn't very well spy on Mrs. Aciddo while they could see her. But this bench had a clear view of Mrs. Aciddo's house, so she'd sit here and wait and try to sort out the new information.

Some of those puzzle pieces were pretty small, but added together they made a pattern. Margo was nervous. Margo wasn't nervous. So Margo wasn't normally nervous, but was yesterday when Jennifer was talking about Mrs. Trax. Why?

If there were a ring of credit card thieves, that meant a lot more than Mrs. Trax and Mrs. Aciddo. Margo too? Could be. And who was in charge?

"I need to talk to Lucas," Jennifer said. There was a quick-stop-and-shop convenience store a block down the street. Jennifer had occasionally used the phone in the open booth in front of the store. She made use of it again, dialing Lucas's number.

"I tried to get you," he said as soon as she identified herself. "I thought we could put a tail on Mrs. Aciddo."

"You did?" Jennifer exclaimed. "But that's what I'm doing."

"You've got a car?"

"No."

"So when she drives to a shopping mall, considering that she does, how are you going to follow her?"

"Oh. I didn't think about following her."

"Jennifer, sometime it might occur to you that we're working this case together." There was a long pause. "I'll be right over. If we're lucky she won't have left yet. See if you can keep an eye on her house."

"She parks her car in front of her house. I've never seen it in the garage. If it's still there, she'll be there."

"Okay. I'll pick you up at the bus stop at the end of the block. Keep your fingers crossed."

Jennifer ran all the way back to the bus stop. Good! Mrs. Aciddo's car was in plain view!

She kept her eyes on it until she was aware that a car had pulled up beside her. "Jennifer," a voice called. "Get in."

She slid into the front seat next to Lucas, who drove just around the corner, where they could watch the

Aciddo house. He turned off the motor, and the old sedan shuddered to a rattling stop.

"I'm glad you're here," Jennifer said. "I was afraid she'd leave before you came."

"She might not leave at all. Or she might go out late this afternoon."

"What would we do?"

"Wait."

"All that time?"

"I keep trying to tell you that private investigation work and police work have their boring moments. You can't sit here and read a good book or doze off. You have to keep alert, keep your eyes on the house and car, and stay aware of what is going on."

"I want to see Bobbie when they have visiting hours at noon."

"Which is the most important?"

Jennifer slid down a little in the seat. "You make life so aggravating."

"So you've said." He suddenly straightened. "She's coming out of her house."

Jennifer straightened. "She's getting into her car!"

"Jen," he said, "get down—way down so she can't see you."

He pulled a soft, felt-brimmed hat from the backseat and tugged it over his eyes. He held up a map as though he were studying directions.

Jennifer, cramped into a ball, waited.

"All right," Lucas said, turning the key in the ignition. "You can get up now. She just passed us."

He did a fast U-turn and was soon on the street behind Mrs. Aciddo's sedan. "I don't think she'll be aware of being followed," he said, letting a gray sports car come between his car and Mrs. Aciddo's sedan.

"If we had two cars we could do this a lot easier," he said. "I'd be in the front car, you'd be in the car in back, and we'd switch off. It makes it easier, because the person being followed doesn't get suspicious. But since we have only one car to use, we'll hope for a chance to attach a hidden beeper to her car."

Jennifer looked at him. "You mean when she parks?"

"Maybe. Or possibly next time we tail her."

"But that's what we're doing now. Will we need to do it again?"

"Do you think she's going to lead us right to the head of the credit card ring? Think, Jennifer. Don't keep acting on impulse and emotion. We're only guessing that she's in this scam. She might have nothing at all to do with it. We might follow her for a week and come up empty."

"I get so impatient." Jennifer leaned back against the seat.

Lucas's voice was sharp. "Sit up there and keep your eyes open. You can't afford to forget what you're doing in order to feel sorry for yourself."

Jennifer sat upright, gripping the edge of the seat. "You make me so angry!" she snapped.

"I don't mind," he said, "if it gets results."

By the time Mrs. Aciddo had driven into the lot of the mall on Everhart and had parked near the entrance to Dillard's, Jennifer had forced herself to calm down. She wasn't going to let Lucas win this put-down game. She was going to show him she could be as professional as he was. However, she couldn't resist sniping as he turned off the ignition, "You should take better care of your car. It rattles."

"I'll stay here," Lucas told her. "You follow Mrs. Aciddo. Keep your distance, but try to see what she's doing." He handed Jennifer a scarf. "Put this over your hair. Wipe off your lipstick." Jennifer followed his instructions quickly. She had one foot out of the car when he added, "And whatever you do, don't let her spot you."

The mall was doing a typical Saturday business. At first, when she entered Dillard's, Jennifer couldn't find Mrs. Aciddo, but she soon saw her in the sweater department. Mrs. Aciddo was examining price tags. She seemed to find one that satisfied her, gave a quick look at the sweater she pulled from the rack, and took it to the woman at the nearest cash register.

Jennifer pretended to be looking at a sweater, standing so that she could get a clear view of Mrs. Aciddo. The woman had pulled out a credit card and handed it to the salesgirl. Jennifer put the sweater she had been holding back on the rack and moved closer. There were some scarves on the counter. She walked close behind Mrs. Aciddo, looked over her shoulder, and—keeping her back to her—picked up a scarf.

She had been able to see the card as the salesgirl laid it on the counter. It was in someone else's name!

Her fingers trembled as she held up the scarf and examined it.

"Can I help you?"

Jennifer looked up, startled, as the salesgirl stood in front of her. "Uh—no, thanks. It's—uh—the wrong color."

"Can I help you find the right color? We've got lots of scarves in the drawers."

"No. I guess I don't want a scarf after all."

The salesgirl was studying her with such a suspicious look on her face that Jennifer just wanted to get away from her. She turned quickly, bumping into a woman who was walking behind her.

"Oh-oh! I'm sorry! I—"

It was Mrs. Aciddo.

18

Mrs. Aciddo's left her house, but that neighbor's still in her front yard. Too many people around. Too much chance of discovery. I'll wait until tonight.

Saw the Wilcox kid sitting on the bench at the bus stop, but next time I drove by she'd gone. What was she doing here? Maybe I'd better send her a little something more than a phone call. I don't need her in my way.

One down, two down, three down. I think she'll have to be next.

19

Mrs. Aciddo was so busy scrambling to pick up the items that had fallen from her handbag that she didn't look at Jennifer. "Believe me, I'm really sorry," Jennifer said. She turned away quickly, so that when Mrs. Aciddo looked up she wouldn't see her face. She was aware of Mrs. Aciddo grumbling and grunting behind her until she had retrieved the items from her purse and hurried off.

Jennifer's hands trembled, and she knew her cheeks were growing pink. From fear? From excitement? The salesgirl was openly staring at her, and Jennifer knew it would be only a minute before she'd call security. Shoplifter? Pickpocket? No telling what the girl thought she might be.

"Look," Jennifer said to the girl, keeping her back to Mrs. Aciddo, "I would like a scarf after all. Have you got a soft pink one? Or maybe a blue one? I'd like to get something pretty for my grandmother."

It was going to blow most of the small amount of cash

Jennifer had in her wallet, but it didn't matter. Jennifer picked out the scarf, paid for it, and surreptitiously looked around for Mrs. Aciddo. The woman was nowhere in sight.

The salesgirl was still watching her, so Jennifer knew she couldn't wander through the store searching for Mrs. Aciddo. She'd have to report back to Lucas.

"I blew it," she said as she flopped into the car beside Lucas. She tugged off the scarf she'd been wearing and threw it and her package on the seat.

"Tell me about it," he said, so she went over the encounter.

"You did a fairly good job," he said, "for a beginner."

"I what?" Jennifer whirled to face him.

"You got an important piece of information. She was using a credit card with someone else's name on it. And from what you told me, she didn't recognize you."

"But I lost her. I didn't follow through."

"What were you hoping for? A signed confession?"

Jennifer leaned back, clasping her fingers behind her head. "Now I feel better. When you said something nice about me, it was so unreal I couldn't believe it."

He didn't answer, so finally she asked, "Are we going to just sit here?"

"I am," he said. "When she comes out of the mall and gets in her car I'll keep a tail on her. Why don't you catch a bus to the courthouse and visit Bobbie?"

"Don't you need me to help you tail Mrs. Aciddo?"

"Not at the moment. I've attached a beeper to her car."

"Won't she see it?"

"No. It's on the frame of the car, near the rear. There's

a small antenna pointing down, but she shouldn't notice it. Its battery pack ought to last at least five days." He pointed toward the dashboard. "And here's my receiver that will pick up the transmitting signal."

"That means you can't lose her?"

"It means that if I lose visual sight of her car, I can still pick up her direction. So, I'll be taking care of that job, and you can talk to Bobbie. You're her friend. She might come out with something to you that she wouldn't tell anyone else."

"I don't want to be a spy!"

"There's a difference between being a spy and being a detective."

"I'm not so sure," Jennifer said. "What are we doing with Mrs. Aciddo?"

"Go on," Lucas said. "Get over to the jail, or you'll be too late. And remember, you're not there to give Bobbie information. You're there to get information from her. So ask her about people her mother was with often. Boyfriends, and so on. Also, see if she can remember the people in those pictures that were missing. And be careful to keep the credit card scam to yourself."

"Don't you listen to what I'm saying? I'm going there to see my friend!"

"And get information."

Jennifer counted slowly to ten. She had heard it helped in tight situations. It didn't help at all.

"Well?" Lucas asked. "What are you waiting for?"

Jennifer groaned. "I don't like to ask you, but could I borrow a couple of dollars? I spent my money on this scarf for Grannie, and I haven't got enough left to make bus fare."

Lucas fished in his pocket and came up with some

change. He added four ones to it and stuffed it into Jennifer's hand. "You'll need lunch, too," he said.

"I'll pay you back."

"I'll expect you to."

"Will you get in touch with me later?"

"Whenever it works out. Get moving."

Jennifer, grumbling to herself about Lucas, strode through the large parking lot toward the bus stop, running the last few steps to catch the bus going toward Leopard. The bus smelled of exhaust and the accumulated sweat and grime and cheap perfume left behind by countless passengers. It lumbered to each stop as though in doubt it would have enough energy to get there.

Jennifer squirmed in her seat and wished she could shout, "Hurry! I need to see Bobbie!"

When she arrived at the sheriff's office, she found a number of people crowded around the desk. There was a well-dressed woman who mopped at her eyes with a fistful of pink Kleenex, and a waddling girl with greasy hair who looked close to her baby's time of delivery. A woman wrapped in a shawl and a man clutching a battered felt hat sat against the wall like a pair of fat gray dumplings and stared into space as though they'd been waiting patiently for years.

Jennifer skinnied through the group to the desk. Without a word a woman handed her a paper to fill out, then gave her a large, numbered blue plastic card. "These have to be returned when you leave," she said in a monotone. "Nothing can be taken in with you. Please leave all your property at the desk. You'll be given a receipt."

She didn't have much to hand over—just the pad and pencil and the small amount of money from her jeans pockets and the package for Grannie. She walked through a scanner and was led, with a few of the others, into an elevator and up to the fourth floor. There was a small yellow-painted waiting room, trimmed in a mustard yellow. She wondered if that was an attempt to make things look cheerful. Jennifer didn't feel cheerful. She was terrified, especially after the guards on the fourth floor directed her through another metal detector and a heavy, metal door that clanged like doom behind her.

She followed one of the guards down a narrow hallway to a small alcove in which two metal stools were bolted to the floor. In front of each stool was a small, screened window. The well-dressed woman she had seen earlier was seated at one of the stools, talking earnestly to a young woman on the other side. Jennifer could look into the cell unit, which was painted the color of green pea soup. Mustard yellow and pea soup! Some paint salesman must have unloaded some unpopular colors on people whose complaints wouldn't count for anything. She could see four small cells along one side. They opened into a narrow area with a table and benches that must have been designed so that prisoners could stretch their legs. She guessed there were another four cells on this side of the area.

A guard called Bobbie to the window in front of Jennifer. Without any makeup besides a light pink lipstick, Bobbie looked like a stranger. She slumped when she walked, and her eyes were glazed over as though she were looking into another time and space.

Jennifer leaned forward, her hands instinctively reaching out to her friend, but touching only the cold metal screen. She forgot the intimidating guard who stood in the hallway against the wall. She was aware only of Bobbie.

"Hey, you're looking pretty good." Jennifer tried to

sound encouraging. "Do you have what you need? Are they giving you enough food? Is everything all right?"

"They treat us okay," Bobbie said.

"Oh, Bobbie, you won't be here long," Jennifer said.

For an instant Bobbie's eyes sharpened, as though Jennifer had suddenly turned on a light. "You mean it?" she asked. Her eyes dimmed again as she answered her own question. "You're just trying to cheer me up."

"Sure I want to cheer you up," Jennifer said, "but Lucas and I are working hard to clear you."

Bobbie just shrugged.

"Look, we're really trying. He's an ex-cop and knows all sorts of stuff about what to do, so it's not like we're amateurs. He's—"

"I met him," Bobbie said. "He's okay."

Jennifer waited just a minute. "Can you help us, Bobbie?"

"How?"

"For one thing, there are some missing pictures in your house."

Bobbie became alert again. "You were in my house?"

"Yes. And remember those pictures on the wall—all those snapshots of your mother with different people?" As Bobbie nodded agreement, Jennifer added, "Some of them were missing."

Bobbie seemed puzzled. "Which ones?"

"That's what we need to find out. From you. I couldn't bring my note pad with me, but I think I can remember. One of them was in the top row, third from the left."

Bobbie's forehead scrunched into wrinkles, and her eyes squeezed shut. Finally she looked at Jennifer and sighed. "I don't know. I can't remember what picture was where."

"Then just tell me who was in the pictures—everyone you can remember. Maybe we can work it out that way."

"That's tough, too." She sighed. "Well, there were some of Stella with me and with Elton and Darryl, and one each of Stella with Daddy and with Mr. Krambo. And some of her boyfriends, and—"

"Who were her boyfriends?"

"Oh, there were a lot of them. I couldn't begin to remember." Bobbie looked away, and Jennifer had the uncomfortable feeling that Bobbie had suddenly remembered something and was hiding it from her.

"Bobbie?" she asked.

Bobbie shook her head impatiently. "It's no use. Anyhow, you're asking me questions like you were a cop. I thought you were my friend."

"I am your friend. I'm trying to help."

"Then don't ask questions I can't answer. Tell me things. I can't find out anything in here. What have the police been doing? Where are Elton and Darryl? Darryl wasn't at Stella's funeral."

"Darryl's in the hospital. Don't worry, he's going to be all right," Jennifer added quickly.

"What?—How?"

"We don't know. Someone beat him up. Lucas thinks the person who did it thought he'd killed Darryl. Don't tell anyone, because Lucas and the police don't want the person to know Darryl is still alive."

Bobbie's words were barely more than a whisper. "Did Darryl say who did it to him?"

"He won't talk about it. Personally, I think Darryl's covering for Elton, but Lucas said he thinks Darryl won't talk because he's so scared of whoever did it."

Bobbie shuddered so violently that Jennifer half rose

from her chair. "Bobbie! Do you need some water? You look awful! You're so white! Bobbie?"

"I'm okay. Don't make so much noise, or they'll come over to see what's the matter." She leaned as close to the dividing window as she could get. "Jen, listen to me. Go home and forget about all this stuff you're doing."

"I'm not going to forget. I know you didn't murder your—uh—mother, and—"

Bobbie interrupted. "You found that out, too, didn't you? That Stella's not my real mother?"

"Hey, Bobbie, it doesn't matter. What's important is getting you out of here."

"I'll get out. The attorney they assigned to me said if all they had against me was circumstantial evidence, then I had a chance."

"That's not enough. We need to find the actual murderer so there won't be any question that you didn't do it."

"You don't have to find out anything. I'll be okay."

"I don't understand you. We're going to get the answers, and you want me to back off. Why?"

"Just stop," Bobbie said. "I mean it, Jen." She quickly got up from her stool and walked back to the area between the cells, her back to Jennifer.

"Bobbie?" Jennifer called.

The guard stepped up and put a hand on Jennifer's shoulder. "Come with me, please," she said.

Jennifer followed the guard into the small area by the elevators. Her sigh of relief as the metal door shut behind her was so loud, a few people turned to stare. She would hate to be in jail!

She hated to have Bobbie in jail. But she was puzzled. She didn't understand their conversation. Was Bobbie hiding something? Why would she do that? It didn't make sense. And there was certainly no real reason why she wouldn't want Jennifer and Lucas to keep up their work.

As she squeezed into the elevator, a woman next to her was saying to her husband, "Donna doesn't seem the same. She isn't even thinking right."

And he answered, "Her circumstances are different. Naturally her thinking is mixed up."

Jennifer nodded. Of course. That was it. Bobbie couldn't be expected to think things out rationally, not with all the stress she was going through.

She turned in her plastic pass and received her belongings.

What would be the next step? Well, why not check out Margo at LaSalon?

As she reached the outside door, she nearly collided with a pudgy man whose light suit coat was yellowed with sweat. Each stepped sideways to the same side to allow the other to pass, then stepped to the other side at the same time, reaching an impasse.

"Sorry," Jennifer said, for the first time looking at the man in front of her. "Oh! Mr. Biddle," she said.

"Well well well, the young lady who came to see me. Did you have any luck with Crandall and Kline?" He giggled.

"You knew I wouldn't. I didn't have that much money."

"So you found out something useful. Private investigators don't come cheap." He laughed again.

"Excuse me," Jennifer said. She began to move around him, but he asked, "Did you see your friend?"

"Yes," she said. She took another step then stopped and turned toward him again. "Are you going to see Bobbie, too?"

"Me? I have nothing to do with her. No, I've got an appointment in court in a few minutes." He patted the worn leather briefcase he carried. "Got some good pictures of a husband who's going to lose out in a divorce case." He sauntered into the building grinning like the Cheshire cat in the illustration Jennifer had always hated.

She hurried down the steps. She had work to do.

But LaSalon had to wait until Jennifer found something to eat. Suddenly she was so hungry her stomach began to rumble. Again she went to the shop on the corner of Chaparral and bought a sandwich and a Coke. This time she didn't share her food with the gulls, but gulped it as greedily as though she too were a scavenger.

She wiped her mouth on the back of one hand, rubbed her hands down the seat of her jeans, and walked down the street to LaSalon.

The acid odors of highly scented hair spray and sour permanent-wave solution saturated the humid air. Two women sat under hair-dryers at the far end of the room, flipping magazine pages and occasionally shouting fragments of conversation at each other. Alice, wisps of her own hair flying from her elaborate hairdo and beads of sweat on her face, briskly teased the hair of a third customer who sat in the chair by the door.

"Hi," Jennifer said to Alice.

Alice quickly looked up, then back to her customer.

"I'm going crazy right now," she said. "If you want to ask any more questions, you'll have to come back."

"I just—"

"On second thought, don't come back, because it won't do you any good. I don't know any more answers, and

Margo's not here. Picks a Saturday to take off, when she knows that's the busiest day we've got."

"Where did she go?"

"Left a note, just stuck under the door if you can believe it!" She patted her customer's hair with a sure hand and let go with such a long blast of hair spray that Jennifer began to cough. "Said she was going out of town."

Alice whipped off the cape she had tied around her customer's shoulders, took her credit card and slammed it into the machine at the front desk, whamming the handle back and forth as though she were planning to batter the card into pieces. Her voice rose as she handed the card and the slip to the customer and waited for her to sign it. "You look lovely, Mrs. Ellison," she trilled. "See you next Saturday."

One of the hair-dryers shut off, and the customer under it began to wiggle out. Alice sighed. "Here's the note," she said, picking up a piece of notepaper and tossing it toward Jennifer.

Jennifer caught it and stared at it. The scrawly handwriting! The same handwriting that was on the note she had found in Mrs. Trax's house!

"Margo wrote this?" she gasped.

Alice was already on her way to take care of the next customer. "No!" she snapped, pausing only to glare at Jennifer. "Shows just how rude she is, how little she cares about walking out on me on our busiest day! That's not even Margo's handwriting. She got someone else to write that note for her!"

"I wonder who it was."

"Probably the man she went out of town with."

"You know this for sure?"

"Honey, when there's a problem, there's always a man behind it."

"Do you know who the man might be?"

"That I don't know, unless it was that skinny wharf rat I've seen her with."

"What's his name?"

"Don't ask me."

Jennifer held up Margo's note. "Mind if I take this?"

"Take it! Keep it! Have it framed if you want! I've got half a mind to fire Margo when she gets back. It's just so hard to get decent hairdressers with a decent following, and—"

She hurried across the room, muttering to herself.

Out on the street, gratefully taking long gulps of the sea-fresh air, Jennifer tried to think about what to do next.

The handwriting had to be the same as that on the note she had found. And again, it looked so familiar. She'd seen it somewhere else. If she could only remember.

Lucas should know about this. And the other note. It was in her top dresser drawer. It would be a good idea to compare them.

It would be an even better idea to go back to the Trax house as soon as possible and see if she could find anything else written in this odd handwriting. If she could only get in touch with Lucas!

But how could she? Darn! She didn't want to wait.

Jennifer made her mind up quickly. She'd go home and put those notes together, just to make sure the handwriting matched. And she'd try her best to remember where she'd seen that handwriting. If Lucas called her, she'd have something to show him. If he didn't, then she'd visit the Trax house again by herself. Tonight.

A few minutes later, as she came up the walk toward her home, she noticed a small box propped against the house next to the front door. The mailman must have brought a package. The mailbox stood open, so if Grannie had brought in the mail she had missed this.

Jennifer ran up the steps and picked up the package, automatically reading the label.

Her own name and address were on the label, and they were written in that scrawly, scribbled, heavy handwriting.

It was like being dropped into the bay in winter. It was hard for Jennifer to breathe, and her fingers were numb blocks of ice. Unable to think, Jennifer simply reacted and threw the package as far from her as she could.

As it slammed against the curb and bounced into the street, one end ripped off and the package exploded.

The door banged open and Grannie rushed out of the house. "What was that?" she yelled.

Jennifer merely pointed.

"You're shakin'," Grannie said. She touched Jennifer's arm. "It scared you, too, huh?"

"Yes." Jennifer found her voice.

"I don't get it," Grannie said. She squinted, peering toward the remnants of paper and cardboard and glass that littered the street and sidewalk in front of their house. A few neighbors had come from their houses, some of them looking up and down the street in bewilderment. "Did it fall off a truck or what?"

"I—I'm not sure where it came from," Jennifer said. She took a few wobbly steps and managed to walk toward the street. Grannie followed her.

"Looks like part of a bottle," Grannie said as they bent over to examine some of the pieces. "And look here—somethin' leaked out of it."

Jennifer picked up a shard of glass from the dark splatter and smelled it. Rum.

Yo ho ho and a bottle of rum.

"You're still shakin'," Grannie said. She tugged at Jennifer's shoulder. "You're workin' too hard, Jennifer Lee. Goin' to be nothin' but a bundle of nerves if you don't slow down a mite."

Jennifer stood, taking deep breaths to keep from screaming. Finally she said, "I'll clean it up, Grannie."

"Good idea," Grannie said. "Wouldn't want to leave that glass in the street." She headed back toward the house as though the matter were over and settled. The neighbors, their curiosity apparently not strong enough to last, had already disappeared inside their homes.

"Grannie," Jennifer said, hurrying to catch up with her, "this wasn't anything much, not even interesting enough to talk about. We ought to just forget it."

"Fine," Grannie said. "But don't forget it until after you sweep up the mess."

As Jennifer swept the rubble into a dustpan and emptied the dustpan contents into a paper bag, her fear turned to anger against this person who had tried to injure or kill her. She wouldn't let him win.

He hadn't stopped her. He had simply succeeded in helping her make up her mind as to what she really wanted to do.

Tell Lucas about this? No way. After what he had said to Grannie about protecting Jennifer, she'd simply find herself sitting at home while Lucas did the work.

Uh-uh. She was going to the Trax home the minute it got dark. And she was going to hunt for something else that might incriminate the person who wrote those notes.

She was definitely going. Tonight.

20

One little, two little, three little, four little . . . squashed bugs.

Stella, you got greedy.

Darryl, you thought blackmail would get you what you wanted.

Margo, you were scared enough to run off at the mouth.

And Jennifer, poor Jennifer, you just might have got close enough to find out. I couldn't take the chance.

Sorry, Jennifer Lee Wilcox, but I couldn't let you get in my way.

I'll find Stella's handbag. I'm good enough to find it, no matter where she's hidden it.

I'll find it. Tonight.

21

The call came from Lucas while Jennifer was cutting zucchini chunks into a pan of water. She quickly dried her hands on a wad of paper towels and grabbed for the telephone before Grannie could get it.

"Did you see Bobbie?" Lucas asked.

"Yes."

"Well?"

"She didn't tell me anything. She asked questions. No one had told her about Darryl. I thought she deserved to know that, but I told her not to tell anyone."

"I assume you did have enough sense to keep quiet about certain other things?"

She sighed. "Of course I did."

"Did Bobbie remember who was in any of those pictures?"

Jennifer wanted to tell him about her feeling that Bobbie did remember something but had kept it to herself. Forget it. It was only a hunch. She didn't want to disturb Lucas's opinion of Bobbie. "No," she said, and added,

"You know there were an awful lot of those snapshots on the wall, and I couldn't remember just which ones were missing."

"Why are you trying so hard to defend her?"

She sucked in her breath as though he had hit her. He didn't miss a thing. "Don't do that, Lucas! I was just telling you what happened."

"So you didn't find out anything."

She thought about the two notes in which the handwriting matched perfectly and the package label—long blown into nothing but scraps—that had been written by the same person. How could she tell him about the notes and not about the label, too? "What about you?" she countered. "Mrs. Aciddo wasn't shopping all day long, was she?"

"I left the tail a couple of hours ago. I wanted to follow a call I picked up on my police-band radio." He paused. "They found a woman's body floating in the ship channel. It turned out to be Margo Zeitlinger."

It took a moment for what Lucas had said to register in Jennifer's mind. "Margo Zeitlinger? Who is Mar— Oh, no! Lucas! You mean the Margo from LaSalon!"

"Yes," he said.

Now she longed to tell him everything, to pour out what had happened in a rush of words and tears, the way she would if she were a little kid needing to be comforted. But she wasn't a kid. She was old enough to be responsible for her own actions, to make her own decisions.

"Do the police know who killed her?" She could hear the waver in her voice. Lucas had probably picked it up, too.

"Not yet," he answered.

There was a long pause during which Jennifer battled

her feelings, finally blurting out, "Lucas, can we go to the Trax house tonight?"

"I'd have to get permission," he said. "It would be hard to do at this hour, especially since it's Saturday. Courts are closed on the weekends, and we might have trouble hunting up a judge who could issue a search warrant."

"Why do we have to have a search warrant? Don't tell me all private eyes get search warrants."

"Some of them don't, but *we* do. I'm an officer, and I know how much better we'll do the job if we work along with the police."

"You're an ex-cop," she mumbled.

He ignored her. "And if we're dealing with an emergency situation, it would be better to step aside and call in the police to take over."

"Why do we have to go through all that red tape?"

"I thought I'd have got it through your head by this time. We go by the book, Jennifer, because that's the way to do it right. Why do you want to go tonight? What have you got in mind?"

There it was in her lap again. "I just thought we could go through the papers in Mrs. Trax's desk."

"The police have done that pretty thoroughly."

"There could be something they missed, because they didn't know what they were looking for."

"Just exactly what have you got in mind?"

"I just want to look through the papers. When we were there before—" No, she thought. If I tell you about the paper I stuck in my jeans and took away with me, you'll just read me out again. No way. I'll handle it myself. "—we didn't have time to really look through everything."

"This second murder puts a new light on things," he

said. "If it's tied into the credit card scam and the murder of Stella Trax, then we'll have to back off and stay out of the way of the police and FBI. We don't want to cause any problems."

"But clearing Bobbie is more important than anything else!"

"We'll talk about this tomorrow. Not tonight."

She recognized the weariness in his voice. He wasn't a young detective. He wasn't the agile private eye on the movie screen. He was retired, and his arthritis hurt him, and he was awfully stubborn.

"Sometimes I can be right, too," she muttered.

"Jennifer," he said. "You must learn that progress usually comes slowly, step by step. You have to go by the book."

"The book again!" She quickly added, "Sorry, Lucas. I didn't mean to snap at you. I just get—well—"

"Impatient." He finished her sentence. "Good night. I'll talk to you tomorrow."

Jennifer slowly replaced the receiver on the telephone, shaking her head at an invisible Lucas, and said aloud, "By tomorrow, dear old by-the-book Lucas Maldonaldo, I bet I'll have enough information for us to know the answers and get Bobbie out of jail."

Grannie came snuffling into the kitchen. She blew her nose and said, "I just writ a letter to Cousin Tessie, over in Lubbock. Told her about your father and that woman and how I'd have to be lookin' for another place to lay my head afore long. Could be Tessie might be lonely, her bein' a widow now, and will ask me to move in with her."

"Oh, Grannie," Jennifer said. "You don't even like Tessie."

"That's true. She always was mealymouthed, and a downright whimper-whiny when she wanted attention, and I won't say she's improved any as she's got older, but I can't be choosy."

Jennifer put an arm around her grandmother's shoulders. "You don't have to worry about where you'll live," she said.

Grannie let out a long, pitiful sigh. "You're the lucky one who don't have to worry. You'll be married and away come graduation time. By the way, you goin' out with Mark tonight?"

Jennifer shook her head and went back to the zucchini, slapping a lid on the pot and putting it on the stove. "He has the late shift at the supermarket."

Grannie lifted her head and sniffed the air. "Somethin' smells good."

"It's the meat loaf in the oven. Dinner will be ready as soon as Dad and Gloria get here."

"I'd set the table for you, but I've been havin' trouble with my feet again today," Grannie said. "I can help best by just gettin' out of your way." She reached for the nearby pack of cigarettes and had one lit by the time she had left the room.

Jennifer wished everyone would get out of her way. It was hard to wait for dinner to be over and her father and Gloria to settle down in the living room. Grannie joined them, turning on the television and grumbling loudly to herself, "Probably don't even like the same shows as I do."

"Dad, could I borrow your car for a little while?" Jennifer asked.

"Where you off to, hon?"

"Just something about Bobbie that I need to do. Okay?"

"Well, I guess so, hon. You're old enough to know what you're doing."

"Huh!" Grannie said, looking pointedly at Gloria. "Bein' old enough doesn't necessarily mean somebody knows what they're doin'."

"Are your car keys on your dresser, Dad?" As he nodded, she said, "I'll be back soon, I hope."

In just a few minutes she was driving her father's old dark blue pickup truck down Carancahua toward the Trax house.

She slowly drove around the block, studying the house, making sure there was no one around. Mrs. Aciddo was at home, and the lights in the front part of her house were on, but her window shades were down. The other neighbors on the block were either away or behind drawn shades and drapes. She was breathing fast, and her hands were so damp they slipped on the steering wheel; but Jennifer knew she could do it.

She parked the truck on the street behind the Trax house, cutting through the neighbor's yard as she had done before. Somewhere on the block a dog barked, and she stiffened, waiting, sweating, until she realized the dog wasn't barking at her.

Carefully she moved across the backyard of the Trax house, stopping under the window to catch her breath. Inch by inch she raised the window, climbed inside and waited again, listening.

The house was alive with small night movements: the scratching of a tree branch as it moved against the roof in the breeze, the slow drip of a faucet in the kitchen, an occasional pop or creak as the house settled and slept. When Jennifer was satisfied that she was the only one inside the house, she turned and quietly lowered the window back into place. Carefully she loosened the drapes at each side of the window, pulling them together, covering the window so that no one could look in and see her.

This time she had brought a pen-size flashlight. It had a small beam, enough to see what might be in Mrs. Trax's desk, but not enough to attract attention outside the house.

She snapped on the light and made her way to the desk.

"Someone's been here!" she whispered as she stared at the mess of papers scrambled on top of the desk.

Like an instant flash the picture of another desk came into her mind and was gone. "Wait!" she said. "A desk . . . a messy desk—"

The picture came back, and she knew. She knew where she had seen the scrawly handwriting before. On Mr. Biddle's desk.

Jennifer leaned against the wall, trying to think things out. There had been lots of papers on that other desk, all in the same handwriting. It had to be Mr. Biddle's handwriting.

And if so, then it must have been Mr. Biddle who—

She walked to the wall where the framed photographs hung and studied them one by one. She had never paid much attention to them, sometimes noticing when Mrs. Trax had added a new one, sometimes wondering what it would be like to have a photographer in a nightclub come over to take your picture while everyone around stared to see who you were, and the man next to you put an arm around your shoulders and tried to look important. There had been a couple of photos like that. Now there was only one.

And there was a blank space in the bottom row among the ones added during the past couple of years.

Jennifer scrunched up her eyes trying to visualize those pictures, trying to remember if the chubby, bald Mr. Biddle had been grinning cheek-to-cheek with the beaming

Stella Trax. Mr. Biddle with the giggles, with the mean sense of humor, who had sent her on a fruitless trip to the wrong investigators. Mr. Biddle who had a briefcase filled with nasty photographs to speed a divorce, who was hurrying to court.

On Saturday.

Jennifer's head snapped up as though she'd been jerked on a line. Lucas had said the courts didn't operate on the weekends. Mr. Biddle had been lying. Why?

She snapped off the flashlight, trying to think. Alice had said something about a skinny wharf rat. For an instant Jennifer could picture the man she had bumped into coming out of Biddle's office. Somehow he must fit in. The questions led to answers, but the answers led to other questions. She needed to talk to Lucas.

From behind the curtains came the scratching of the window being opened.

Jennifer took a step toward the front door, then realized that whoever was coming in the window would hear the door being opened and would go after her. Frantically she watched a hand grabbing the curtains, pushing them aside, as a man's leg was thrown over the sill.

It took only seconds to squeeze past the rickety end table to a spot behind the large armchair that stood askew in the corner of the room, the corner nearest the kitchen. The ceramic lamp on the table wobbled as her feet caught in the lamp cord, then settled back into place. She breathed shallowly as she heard a thump, then footsteps in the room. Someone walked close to the chair and entered the kitchen. She could hear a drawer being opened and closed. A beam of light drew a wide yellow circle on the floor. The circle came near, sweeping across the floor.

From her hiding place Jennifer watched the track of

the beam until it hit the mirror on the far wall and reflected the man who was holding Stella Trax's flashlight.

It was Elton Krambo.

Jennifer weakly leaned against the wall, relieved that it was only Elton. And she'd been so frightened. She didn't like Elton, but at least she didn't have to be afraid of him now that she knew Mr. Biddle was the dangerous one.

She had put her hands on the floor, ready to climb out of her hiding place, when she heard a voice from the direction of the window. "Just keep those hands up nice and high, Elton. If you move I'll shoot you."

Some grunting and puffing followed. Jennifer knew that Mr. Biddle was climbing into the room.

Elton didn't answer. Soon there was a thump as Mr. Biddle landed on the floor.

"You knew about the window," Elton said.

"So did you, apparently."

"I used to live here. I have a right to be here."

"I have a right, too," Mr. Biddle said. "Stella seems to have hidden some property of mine. Maybe you've seen it. I think it's inside a very large handbag." His voice became taut as a line holding a five-pound fighting snapper. "Or maybe that's also what you're here for—the handbag."

"Look," Elton said, "we understand each other. I even did time without giving away your game. I'm not about to undercut you. Whatever you want the handbag for, that's your business. I want it for the money and bankbooks that are in it. You know Stella. She kept everything of value in that handbag."

"You're asking me to trust you, Elton? Well, for the moment I will." Mr. Biddle snickered as though that were a huge joke. "Suppose we look for that handbag together."

"Fair enough," Elton said.

"Where do you suggest we look?"

"I wish I knew. Stella used all sorts of tricks to keep us from spying on her."

"Not very clever, were you? Well, a woman usually keeps her handbag nearby. I'm guessing on her bedroom."

"I don't think so," Elton said. "I think we should look in the kitchen."

The flashlight moved toward her, and Jennifer squatted back against the wall, behind the protection of the broad chair.

"Better yet. I have a flashlight too, so I'll search the bedroom and you look through the kitchen."

Jennifer watched Elton's legs move past her. He was in the kitchen only a few seconds when there was a thump and a curse.

Biddle ran from Stella's bedroom into the living room, calling in a low voice, "What was that? What happened?"

"Damn cockroach," Elton grumbled. "The kitchen's full of them."

"Keep it down," Biddle said. "The place belongs to them, too." Jennifer heard his giggle fading down the hallway.

If she could get Elton out of the way, she could reach the kitchen telephone and try to call Lucas. How could she do it? She shifted position, careful to avoid the lamp cord.

The lamp cord.

Silently she unplugged the cord. She could see, from the glow of the flashlight, that Elton's back was toward her as he squatted, going through the lower kitchen drawers.

She would have to be fast. She couldn't make a sound.

Silently, Jennifer got to her feet, grasped the lamp around its neck, slid from the place behind the chair, took two quick steps toward Elton, and brought the base of the lamp down on his head.

Elton fell forward against the drawers. There was a thump, but Jennifer hoped Mr. Biddle would think Elton was after another cockroach. She lowered Elton to the floor. He was breathing steadily, and his head wasn't bleeding. She hadn't wanted to hurt him, but she didn't have a choice. Maybe he'd come to. What then?

Jennifer knew that Mrs. Trax hung an apron in the kitchen closet, so she pulled it out and bound Elton's hands behind him with the ties of the apron.

The telephone was on the side counter. Crouching, as though she were being watched, she ran to the phone. Using the penlight in fingers that were trembling so much she could hardly aim it, she dialed Lucas's number.

As she waited, automatically counting the rings, she began to realize that Lucas wasn't going to answer his telephone. Wasn't he there? Was he asleep? Oh, Lucas! You've got to answer!

But the phone rang on unheeded.

She had one other chance. She hung up and quickly dialed the operator.

After the third ring the operator answered, and Jennifer whispered, "Let me have the police! Quickly!"

"I'm sorry," the operator said. "I can't hear you. Can you speak a little more loudly?"

"The police!" Jennifer's whisper was only a little louder.

"I'm sorry. I can't hear you."

"Hang up, please." The voice, close to her ear, came accompanied by a blinding light as Mr. Biddle's flashlight was aimed at Jennifer's eyes.

Jennifer did as he said and threw up an arm to ward off the glare.

The flashlight lowered. She could see Mr. Biddle studying her. "Apparently you didn't get my little gift," he said.

She didn't answer.

"A dud?" he said. "I don't usually make mistakes like that."

He waited for Jennifer to reply, but she simply stared at him.

He chuckled. "Looks as though Elton is going to wake up with a very sore head. Did you really think that desperate act would help you?"

Jennifer heard a car pull up outside the house. Rubber sliding against the curb. Neighbors coming home? Another car soon followed. A lower-pitched motor. The tiniest of rattles as the engine shut off.

She wanted to shout. She recognized the sound of Lucas's car. What was he doing here? Did he know she'd come to the Trax house? And why two cars?

With the curtains over the back window Lucas and whoever was with him would be unable to see Mr. Biddle. Mr. Biddle with the gun in his hand.

The switch to the light over the sink was next to the telephone. If she turned on the light, whoever was out there would be alerted.

"Nothing to say?" Mr. Biddle said. "Well, I suppose you're right. It's time for you to join our friend down on the floor."

Elton groaned and opened his eyes, blinking as though caught in the middle of a dream.

"You're a liability, Elton," he said. As he pointed his gun toward Elton, Jennifer whirled, snapped on the light, and dove to one side, rolling under the kitchen table.

She heard a shot and the slapping, splintering of wood near her head. There was a rush of noise that hammered against her ears and sparks that burned black and zoomed into a tunnel. Jennifer whirled into the darkness with them.

She awoke to find herself stretched out on the kitchen floor. In front of her face was the back of a pair of men's shoes. The shoes took a step away from her.

Jennifer struggled to sit up.

"She's come out of it," a deep voice said from across the room.

The shoes—with pants legs attached—turned toward her. Lucas bent down. "You're all right," he told her. "Think you can get up, or do you need a hand?"

Jennifer took a couple of deep breaths. The room and the people in it became real, and she remembered.

"Lucas!" she said, stumbling to her feet, wishing she weren't so off-balance and clumsy. "You're all right! Did the others—?"

"No shots fired," he said. He looked toward the splintered table leg and added, "Except for the one aimed at you."

He reached out a hand, and she grabbed it, steadying herself. "Biddle and Elton Krambo are in custody," he said. "Elton's asking to plea bargain already. I think he'll give the police and FBI quite a bit of information."

"I have to tell you something!" Jennifer said.

"You don't need to tell me. It's pretty obvious what happened, from the moment your voice gave you away and I realized you were coming here no matter what I said."

"That's not what I want to tell you. I want you to

know that you're not the only one who knows how to listen. I learned, too. That's how I knew it was your car outside. The rattle!" She waited a moment. "Well, aren't you proud of me?"

"Proud of you? For not following orders, for endangering your life, for taking unnecessary risks, for—?"

Jennifer pulled the notes with Mr. Biddle's handwriting from her back jeans pocket. "Here," she said. "That note that's supposed to be from Margo. It's in Mr. Biddle's handwriting. I've even found evidence for you!"

Lucas pulled out two of the wooden kitchen chairs. "Sit down," he said. "Carl and the others will be wanting to talk to you when they're ready. You can turn over your evidence to them."

"They'll ask me what happened?"

"Every detail. And when they're through with their interrogation they'll chew on you for getting in their way and for doing all the things you did that they'll think were pretty dumb."

"But we helped prove that Bobbie didn't kill Mrs. Trax! That's what counts!"

Maybe it was the way Lucas looked at her. Maybe it was the overloud echo of her words. Tears began to spill down her cheeks as she faced the knowledge she had forced to the back of her mind.

Lucas handed her a clean handkerchief. "I don't suppose you have one of your own."

Jennifer shook her head, and he added, "Bobbie didn't kill Stella Trax, but I imagine you've figured out by now that she did know what Stella was up to. I doubt that Bobbie had been told who was involved in the scam, but I think it will come out that she did help in passing counterfeit cards at the stores."

Jennifer rolled into a ball of misery, crying until her

sobs were only dry gulps. Finally she said, "I knew when I realized that Mr. Biddle had gone to see Bobbie. It all added up." She leaned back in her chair and looked at Lucas. "But I didn't really want to know."

"It's tough now," he said, "but you'll get over it."

"I don't think I ever will."

"You learn to," he said. One corner of his mouth turned up as he added, "When you're a cop."

"I'm not a cop!"

"Have you thought about becoming one? You're pig-headed and lippy, and you don't even know what the word *patience* means, but I think you're smart enough to learn to do things right."

"Are you crazy?"

"Think about it. Take a couple of years at Del Mar College, then try the academy entrance exam. I believe you've got what it takes."

"I haven't got enough money to go to college, and I'm supposed to get married after I graduate in May."

"I'll ask around. We ought to be able to come up with a scholarship for you. And you're much too young to get married. Put that out of your mind."

"Do you really think you have a right to tell me what to do with my life?"

"You're a fine one to talk about rights." He actually smiled at her.

"It isn't just what I want to do," she said. "What about Mark? I wouldn't want to hurt Mark."

"You'll hurt him more if you marry him just because you think it's expected of you."

Jennifer snapped, "Now you sound like a marriage counselor!" But she was surprised to find that mixed with the sorrow and exhaustion was a comforting touch of relief.

"With a part-time job and a scholarship you could manage it," Lucas said. "Probably even handle an apartment of your own."

Jennifer didn't want to think about Lucas's idea, but her mind swooped after his words like a gull after a fish. "Maybe," she said aloud, "Grannie and I could—" She shook her head and quickly added, "I'm not saying your idea is any good. I have to give it a lot of thought, and right now I hurt inside and I don't even want to think about it."

Three men came into the kitchen. One of them was Detective Carl Robbins. "Young lady—" Carl began, but Lucas held up a hand.

"Jennifer has got some evidence to give you. Biddle made a careless mistake, and it's going to cost him in the Zeitlinger murder. You might want to congratulate her."

"Congratulate her! When she—"

Lucas interrupted. "She'll learn to do it right next time. We've been talking about her spending two years in junior college, then trying out for a class at the police academy."

"Are you crazy, Lucas!" But the detective's scowl turned into a smile, and he began to laugh. "If she can obey orders for even one week I'll eat my badge!"

"I'll buy the ketchup," Lucas said. "Now treat this future officer kindly, and let's get down to business."

Whatever I decide, I hope Mark will understand, Jennifer thought, but she put Mark out of her mind as she tugged her notebook out of her pocket and asked, "Where do you want me to start?"